Boiled Americans

Michael Allen Rose

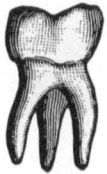

Bizarro Pulp Press
an imprint of JournalStone Publishing

Bizarro Pulp Press books may be ordered through booksellers or by contacting:

Bizarro Pulp Press, a JournalStone imprint
www.BizarroPulpPress.com

ISBN: 978-1-942712-48-0

Printed in the United States of America
JournalStone rev. date: July 13, 2015

Cover Art: Matthew Revert
Interior Formatting: Lori Michelle
www.theauthorsalley.com

To Sauda, for holding me
up above the surface.

Dedicated to all the
victims and those lost in
time.

[A note for new recruits on the filing system: The Master Number 22 carries the energies and attributes of diplomacy, intuition and emotion, balance and harmony, adaptability, personal power, redemption, idealism, expansion and evolution, philanthropy, service and duty and **manifesting your highest ideals and desires***. Number 22 is a number of power and accomplishment.]*

There is a 100% chance that you will walk outside of your home this afternoon and be shot. It will happen. Do not question this wisdom. Embrace it. Reset. Rewind your mind. The air is filled with springtime and bullets. Every child is a bomb, and every house pet is a scimitar. Every mailbox holds the potential of a million letter bombs.

There are forces watching you right now, forces waiting to harm you, forces you don't understand. They have no motivation but blood, no hunger but tears. No patience. No pity. They will follow you home at night, and put bullet holes in your family and possessions and everything you enjoy. They survive, like roaches, and feed on your discarded thoughts of violence and apathy.

But, don't be afraid.

Don't fret, now. Breathe. Everything is fine. Remember, you're an American. Even if you aren't an American, you're an American. Trust me. That's the American way. We will assimilate you, regardless of whether you want us to or not. Our methods range from immigration to naturalization to subjugation. We learn from our history. Illegal immigration started in 1492, true, and we did it first and best. We can rape the citizenship right into your prefrontal cortex. Relax. We'll waive your rights for you. You're no longer a dull, mundane, ineffective "person." You are now an American colony. Congratulations! Colonies have rights. Corporations are people. Certainly to a greater degree than people are people. And they're bullet-resistant. So calm down, take my hand, let's read the crime report together:

```
Case File 001

A weather report from The Chicago Tribune July
7th, 2014:

Friday's 4th of July weather couldn't have
```

been nicer. 98% of the day's possible sun
poured down on the area, making it one of the
3 sunniest Independence Days of the past 15
years.
Over the course of 84 hours during the
Independence Day holiday in Chicago, from 3:30
p.m. Thursday to 3:30 a.m. Monday, 82 people
were shot and 14 were killed.

I know.

There are a lot of numbers.
I know, there are a LOT of numbers. Perhaps it would be best to take notes.

Chance of earthquakes: [REDACTED]
Lake breezes are history this weekend; south/southwest winds are to defeat "lake cooling" spreading warmth up to and over area beaches.
The number of dead could rise because several of the injured are listed in critical condition. Five people were reportedly shot by Chicago police and two died.
The frequently chilly spring and early summer "onshore" (easterly) breezes, which sweep off Lake Michigan's chilly waters, prove the bane of the beachgoer and warm weather enthusiast's existence in spring and early summer.
"Chicago's violence problem is largely a gun problem," according to a May proposal to toughen the city's gun laws. "Every year, Chicago police officers take thousands of illegal guns off the street. But, despite these efforts, it remains far too easy for criminals to get their hands on deadly weapons."
The average body temperature of a person who has just been shot is 98.6 degrees Fahrenheit.
At room temperature, the temperature of the body will drop about 34°F in the first hour after death, and between 33° and 35°F each hour after that. The core body temperature of the deceased will often be taken as soon as possible at the scene, either using a rectal thermometer or a reading from the liver.
Cool easterly winds, often dubbed "lake breezes" or "lake winds", come ashore in two ways—first, with organized northeast or easterly

winds off Lake Michigan or, secondly, as more "localized" (i.e., limited coverage) easterly late morning and afternoon winds with an impact limited to the lakeshore or a limited distance inland—sometimes as little as a few city blocks.

All gunshot wounds can be divided into four types:
- Contact: A shot in which the muzzle of the gun was applied to the skin and fired.
- Close-Range: The muzzle of the gun was 6-8 inches away from the skin.
- Intermediate Range: The gun muzzle was 8 inches to 3.5 feet away from the skin.
- Distant: The gun was over 3.5 feet away from the skin.

At least 30 people were shot over 13 hours starting 2:30 p.m. Sunday afternoon, and continuing into early Monday morning. Out of those 30, 4 have been declared dead, and several more remain in critical condition.

The risk of severe weather will increase later this weekend.

Oh, yes, it will grow. The rain is bullets.

Saturday's quiet weather regime belies the more active pattern predicted to take shape later this weekend.

Surging temperatures and humidities[1] Sunday interacting with an unseasonably strong and southward-displaced jet stream will produce clusters of strong, possibly severe thunderstorms later Sunday night. Hand-in-hand with the severe weather risk later this weekend is the potential for heavy, thundery downpours predicted to erupt in Sunday's warm, humid environment—particularly later in the day and/or at night.

With the ground saturated in many parts of the Chicago area, heavy rainfall later this weekend would cause problems and will have to be monitored.

Fourteen were killed.

Continue to monitor the weather. Continue, or we'll shoot.

But wait, before we begin, before I tell you about Segundo Morris and the cops and the doomsday preppers, we have a task to complete.

I spin the cylinder. I hold my arm straight. I pull the trigger.

---

[1] Humilities and humanities are similarly reacting, however in a different phase.

Michael Allen Rose

P   U   L   L   *click-*BANG*

by echos off

event, followed

pressure

extreme high

short duration

by a very

characterized

wave,

complex

a   100dB

every surface nearby. Unprotected, the ear drum smashes into the anvil of the ear ∎∎∎

which   100dB

crashes

to a stop

against it's

supporting

structures.

The sound

pressures

exceed a

whopping

100 dB

BANG!!!!!!!

Watch for it. Duck when necessary.

I. Resume Panel Beatings

I have my lips sewn together, but my eyes are propped wide open like Uncle Sammy's rosy-cheeked asshole.

I feel it begin again and it can't stop. Can't stop. Can't stop. My teeth grip the rebar. They crack and ideas fall out. Is this what you think it is? If it isn't, what is it?

That child brought a sandwich to school shaped like a gun. "You can't close Guantanamo!" he screamed. The administrators didn't know what to do, so they recorded it all on the audio-visual equipment. "It's the guantanamostest! It's more fun than spending a summer at concentration camp! More thrills than the rides at the industrial park! Don't be such a suicide bummer!"

My only response is magic: Bake me into a mad cosmic pie, teeming with hordes of tiny brain-spiders. I emit the endless miasma of a blocked writer, clearing out the refuse and letting loose with a string of gibberish, senseless and wasting the moment.

Freeze frame flash of nothing, cicadas screaming to the high heavens without vacancy. A sea of smiles provide examples yet I find myself uneasy to imitate, fearful my face will crack into shattered elevator glass.

A room of beautiful women with no faces. Neon remembrance. Clocks spin wildly, out of control. The door opens wide, spewing a cloud of archaic odors and patchouli stench. A little girl smiles and dances across the sidewalk. I suddenly find myself smiling at the hope of a brighter future. Not for me, but for someone.

Case File 002

• A 24-year-old man was shot to death about
2:20 a.m. at 84th Street and Buffalo Avenue in
the Bush neighborhood on the South Side. He
was found in the middle of the block with
multiple gunshot wounds. Police believe his
attacker approached from a gangway and opened
fire.

The man, a typical American, according to the
Cook County medical examiner's office, was
pronounced dead at the hospital early Monday
morning. The aspirin they prescribed did not
cure his gunshot wound. He had blue eyes and
blonde hair, the classic Scandinavian look
with broad shoulders. He had spent the last
several hours at the florist where he'd been
picking out a bouquet for his lover[2]. His socks
had a design that reminded him of swarming
flies.

---

[2] For the lover: An objectification serenade. I will sew us together, eyes shut, lips
apart, a single needle, shared, violet thread shredding holes in our skin. I pull tight
and we collapse into each other.

II. ENG 501: Approaches to Metafiction

I **will never** write the great American novel. I am not Ernie Hemingway. I am not Willie Faulkner or Nate "Scooter" Hawthorne. There are books out there—hunted in the wilderness, hiding in the aisle between the coffee bar and the desktop bobbleheads—books that describe in great and lurid detail the intricacies of plot and structure. They contain the Lazarus effect, ancient secrets of breathing life into dead character. Thematic swaths of devastation culled with the scythe of linguistic excellence fall from between their pages like fresh rain on a field of skulls.

This is not the great American novel. Teach this in English literature classes in any major American high school and you'll be pushed into a pit of tigers and punji sticks. The characters are not a subset of demonstrable demographics, squeezing out raw dialogue pleasing to the ear like half-remembered music. There are no parameters fencing in the thematic resonance. No meaning spared the counter-revolutionary stare of Stalin's winter. Likeable protagonists are you and me, and nobody else, but these words will not teach you more about yourself, not directly, not explicitly.[3]

Instead, this book has a cast of millions. All the plots ever made, whole and placed in the front yard of your massive superego mindslave like a garden gnome in Siberia. There's a fisherman, and a headmistress, some zoo animals, and some shadows. Everyone you know is here; you are here, I am here, and Segundo Morris, that rakish rapscallion—even he is here.

---

[3] "If everyone thinks I'm so great," said the protagonist, "how come it gets so quiet in here whenever I stop talking?"

Segundo Morris survived the Declension. Now what?

Now we focus in, we shrink our view.

Let the lens crack and the heavens burst.

Let our optic nerves be severed and our severed sense of selves be nervous.

The cast is huge, but I will hold your hand like an usher assisting an elderly theatre patron. I will be your hearing aid. I will underline the important players in the program for you, and together we shall sit quietly and watch it all unfold. Reverse origami. The shape of a trigger. The bang.

Every word is a bullet plunged into your sick hole cell anemic human shell casing.

The author is dead.[4]

The author is no longer in control of this manuscript.[5]

The author might enjoy being flogged. Do not judge, footnote

The author is Segundo Morris.[6]

---

[4] The author is fine. It's only the concept of authorship that is dead. The author is a liar.

[5] The author deserves to be flogged.

[6] Then, the author is dead after all.

Boiled Americans

Case File 003

• A woman, 44, was killed at 12:30 a.m. Monday in the Morgan Park neighborhood on the Far South Side. She was shot in the torso and arm while standing against a car on the 10900 block of South Throop Street. It's not clear whether she was the target. Investigators at the medical examiner's office aren't sure who she is. They believe she is a typical American, a light-skinned black woman with close-cropped hair. She had spent most of the afternoon drinking coffee with a friend and complaining about her impending evaluation at work.[7] Her breath smelled like lilac.

---

[7] I recently experienced a work review in which I received average marks and a written report based on errors made. I received twenty bullets per bullet wound, metaphorically/metaphysically. More on that later, when the aspirin have kicked in and the pain in my leg has begun to dissipate. (And now to Segundo Morris, with the weather!)

III. Mugger Parties

Did I ever tell you about the time I got mugged?Inventory: iPod with headphones in top left jacket pocket. Wallet with a few bills in right front pocket. Cell-phone in left front pocket. Business cards behind iPod in top left jacket pocket. Brown leather gloves in lower jacket pockets. Halloween 2011. Chilly. Evening. Dark blue sky, just next to black. Walking alone on the north side. On my way to a Halloween party. Angled street. Mostly white neighborhood. Kids running down the street together and people walking dogs had been seen only minutes before. Feelings of relative safety.

The big guy was walking slightly behind two other guys on a sidewalk suddenly emptied of everyone but us. As I walked toward them, he moved to intercept. I moved to the side, and he mirrored me. Some animal part of me kicked against the cage and awoke the follicles on the back of my neck.I was still planning to move to the side. The rational part of me knew that this was ridiculous. The two guys in front of him kept walking, he slowed."Give me your shit." He grabbed the collar of my brown coat and pulled me in close. He must have seen the confused irritation on my face. "Give me your shit!""I don't have any shit!" I brought my arms up and pushed his hands off my body.

Act without hesitation.

He picked up a bottle and held it up next to my head as he grabbed my collar again. "Give me your shit. I'll break this bottle in your fucking face."He was breathing heavily, ragged. He was nervous, his energy and adrenaline carrying him through his threat. I pushed him off me again. "Fuck you, I don't have any shit."

Act without hesitation. Hesitation will get you killed.

10

Boiled Americans

He threw the bottle down against the street, where it shattered. It was loud, but muffled by the blood in my ears. He grabbed me again; I pushed him off again and stepped away, in the direction I was originally headed. "You stupid fucker," I said, "I'm going to call the cops on your ass." In my mind, it was ludicrous that I was being mugged. Seriously? This is ridiculous. I'm not being mugged. That's just dumb.

```
Act without hesitation. Hesitation will
   get you killed. In a fight to the
death, you must be prepared to resist
      with everything you have.
```

He looked at me like I was crazy. He was gauging the level of my insanity against his own. Two animals sniffing, posturing, rooting. He hesitated, then he backed up a step or two. I did the same as I pulled out my phone, looking at him like he was a figment of my imagination. He had made up his mind. He looked at me like I was too much trouble. He looked at me like I was insane. He began to jog away. The last I saw of him, he'd almost caught up to the duo that had been walking with him before.

```
Control the weapon. Counter-attack. The
   weapon is fear. No matter what the
    weapon is, the weapon is fear.
```

A shake stepped into my shoes, a tremor, a shudder, a ghost of possible futures. I walked on. I walked faster. It didn't occur to me until later, when I was recounting the story to my friends, that the situation could have gone much worse for me. The guy had fifty pounds on me, easy. He was obviously motivated to take whatever valuables I had. He was dangerous. He wasn't crazy enough.

```
Break joints. Use leverage. Induce
              pain.
```

I like to think that just as I had gone off to a party with improvisers, theatre technicians, and performance artists, he had gone off to a mugger party. I like to picture them sitting around drinking and chatting, all in costumes, and my mugger was super depressed. He was saying things like, "I don't know, you guys. I really don't know if I'm cut out for this stuff." Then, his friends, the other muggers, would comfort him. "You just had a bad night, man. You're a great mugger. Come on, don't let one bad experience ruin your mugging career." Maybe he was consoled by this. Maybe he rededicated himself to the art and science of mugging people.

My fight or flight mechanism is set permanently on "resist in disbelief."

Boiled Americans

• A 23-year-old man was shot to death at 9:05 p.m. Friday at 116th Street and Stewart Avenue in the West Pullman neighborhood on the Far South Side. He had been on a porch when someone opened fire, wounding the man. According to the medical examiner's office, the victim is a typical American. He enjoyed the occasional cigar. Sometimes he drank milk straight from the carton. He'd once lost a hundred dollars in a game of dice, and his wife hit him with an ironing board. They made up later that night over a bottle of wine and some TV on the couch. When shots were fired, neighbors at the house next door had been playing cards—their game lit by lights attached to an umbrella set up over a table. They dropped to the ground and crawled inside. The wounded man ran through a vacant lot and collapsed in a bush-like patch of weeds growing under a light pole. Police found him bleeding from at least two gunshot wounds to his torso and he was taken to Advocate Christ Medical Center. While a single squad car guarded the scene where the man fell, someone opened fire at 11:05 p.m. a block away at 115th Street and Harvard Avenue, wounding another typical American who later turned up at Roseland Community Hospital with a gunshot wound to the left side of his chest. The 20-year-old man, who was an avid fisherman and occasional drunk, was dropped off at the hospital with the wound at 11:20 p.m. He had forgotten to buy milk at the corner store, and his cereal would go dry the next morning.

IV. A list of things that are broken:

- **Weather**. Did you know it rained frogs in Ishikawa Prefecture, Japan, once? Also, in Rákóczifalva, Hungary, It's rainin' frogs. Hallelujah.
- Children. They were not firing rockets. They were playing. One had a Captain America shield painted on the lid of a metal garbage can. He blew his proverbial fingers off.
- God. My God is better than your God, therefore I'm better than you. He'd tell you himself but he is conspicuously missing. Leave a message after the crucifixion.
- Nutrition. Vitamins. And minerals. And fatty deposits. And carbohydrates. And calories. Gluten free Africans are bad for your teeth.
- Time. It seemed to go faster and faster as we grew older and older until we no longer had any sense of its passage. Lifetimes were individual ticking minutes on a broken sundial.
- Speed. It's much too fast. It's also too slow. It burns through the atmosphere with reckless abandon for the participation medal of velocity being awarded to those of us who misconstrue our own physics.
- Dream. Wakeful nightmare piss in your sheets magic hour fragile glass shattering light candle burning at both ends.
- Light. Blind people change light bulbs through osmosis. You can't see what you can't eat and then you can't remember it.
- Travel. The cars are stopped, waiting for a train. Each driver has thick leather cords sewn through each eye lid. They all have that new car smell. Roadkill travel brochures.
- Race. Post-racial society tells me that I should stop reading *Better Homes and Gardens* because the pages are too white, but then

that kid who died choking on justice tells me that the sunbeams are made of devils and the bullets are free. I don't know what color to believe anymore, but I do know that the octoroons and the mulattos have banded together to form a new tribe of man-shaped holes in the scenery.

- Pets. If cats had opposable thumbs and could speak English, they would rule the world ten times over. Build a strong back for your future in the catnip mines.

V. The further adventures of Segundo Morris, lightning space-boy.

[STATIC]

[VERTICAL HOLD]

When last we left our intrepid young heroin, he was fingering a mute. After beating words to death with a shovel, his ship crash-landed on the planet Metatron. There, he met with Frank Frankerson, a man who can only derive sexual pleasure from wearing an ape suit and humming. They walked the streets together and ran into a prostitute that looked suspiciously like Benito Mussolini in a toga. Segundo's lips fell off when he realized his sudden yearning for ice cream, so he and the prostitute stole a 1972 Gremlin and set out for Cincinnati, leaving Frank to his own devices. Unfortunately, Frank had anticipated this double-cross and filled the trunk with melted butter. This depressed our hero and took him back to a memory from his childhood, when he was attacked by his hairdresser for whistling at an onion. The prostitute filled his shoes with gelatin and rode off into the sunset whistling the theme to "Django." We now join our hero, already in progress . . .

[TEST FREQUENCY]

Segundo Morris unholsters his international galactic underblaster and fires at the space mosquitoes! They explode in furious lightshow crackles and change into chairs. "There are never enough chairs in space!" declares our hero, heroically.

Suddenly, the evil Doctor Shap-Mung turns up! What's he doing here? "I've infected your television monitor screens with radical viruses, you filthy space-boy! Now my obviously evil plans will finally come to fruition!"

Suddenly! A broadcast!

"This is the voice of Asteron. I am an authorised representative of the Intergalactic Mission, and I have a message for the planet Earth. We are beginning to enter the period of Aquarius and there are many corrections which have to be made by Earth people. All your weapons of evil must be destroyed. You have only a short time to learn to live together in peace. You must live in peace... or leave the galaxy."

Segundo Morris turns to the camera and puts his hands on the sides of his face like the infamous child in Home Alone who isn't dead now (maybe) but wishes he was (maybe). Doctor Shap-Mung stares into the camera. His gaze does not quiver, does not break. The pupils of his eyes begin to shudder like they are being vibrated in a paint-can shaker. The camera zooms in so the screen is filled with his eyes and nothing else.

Segundo Morris shouts from somewhere off-screen. "I'm off to save the universe, thanks to the power of media intervention!" The sound effects man makes whooshing sounds with his mouth; they are entirely unconvincing.

But on the screen: the eyes of Doctor Shap-Mung. Creases at each edge suggest that he is smiling, as his pupils begin to liquefy. They drop like two ink spots down through the irises and past the bottom whites into the skin folds underneath each eye.

The transmitter for your program tonight is beyond the capabilities of the usual UHF culprits.

Soon, his irises follow suit, glistening as they pool into liquid, like oil dropped into a cup of water, and slide down the white as the tiny capillaries retract and curl. The whites remain, but as the show continues, boys and girls, watch for secret messages!

The whites blink off-white, and then bright white, like there is a lighthouse inside the skull of Doctor Shap-Mung. The code it spells out tells you the date of your death.

VI. Fish Story

Then I see this here fish, sittin' up in this tree. Don't trust him none at all. I'm gonna watch me this goddamn fish, just to see what he does. See me a banyan tree not thirty yards from where that goddam fish is bidin' his time, so I strap my pack real tight and climb right up in them branches, all the while keepin' an eye on that goddam fish. All the sudden like, I stay real still 'cause I notice he's starin' right back at me. Thing about it is, fish ain't got good eyesight, and fish ain't got good memory neither, so if'n I stay stock still long enough, that goddamn fish might just forget I'm here. His big ol' dinner plate sized fish eye is beady as all hell, wide open like a blue moon. I'm holdin' my breath til' my heartbeat fills my ears with fluid. That goddam fish, he stops lookin' my way and yawns real big, showin' off them needle sharp teeth of his. Reckon he might be showin' off now, peacockin' as it were. I ain't intimidated and I ain't fooled. If that fish thinks he's gonna' get away with whatever it is I reckon he's up to, he's got another thing comin' for sure. An earthquake's comin.' These here bones don't lie.

VII. The Conspiracy Theory to End All Conspiracy Theories: A Conspiracy

The WTO does my taxes every year! The trilateral commission gives me greasy hand-jobs in the back rooms of the Pentagon!

MI6 is working with the People's Democratic Republic of China to abolish free thought by overloading cellphone towers with sodium pentathol!

Not only that, but the Republican Party and the Libertarians are working together to infect the country's water supply with secret agents and the Bilderberg Group's black ops teams, in order to establish a totalitarian World Government! Furthermore, the combined forces of the Rosicrucian Fraternity and the Reptilian Council are plotting to immanentize the Eschaton by weakening wheat farms with hypnotic suggestions!

The Communist Party has teamed up with the ghost of Robert Anton Wilson, and they plan to prevent the creation of a utopian World Government by filling our bodily fluids with testosterone.

NASA and the Church of Scientology are working together to overload the government's computer databases with Chemical X, in order to prevent the creation of a utopian World Government! Just imagine the public outcry if it came to light that the combined forces of the Moonies and the Cthulhu cult are plotting to abolish free speech by undermining our brains with saccharin!

The Bavarian Illuminati has teamed up with Elvis Presley, and they plan to resurrect Lenin by infesting the nation's livestock farms with nanomachines, while the combined forces of the Black Hand and Opus Dei are plotting to prevent the Singularity by subverting the moon with fluoride!

I must survive to cast a light on these terrible shadows! The people must know the Order of the Knights Templar is working with the CIA to prevent the Singularity by polluting ATMs with nanomachines and Red #4!

The Trilateral Commission is going to use demon blood to pollute our bodily fluids, in order to destroy the Free Market. The Ordo Templi Orientis is planning to pollute airports with LSD in order to turn the populace into mindless drones. Perhaps the fact that the Tea Party and Al-Qaeda are working together to weaken the major credit-card companies with asbestos, in order to prevent human contact with enlightened extra-terrestrials, will alarm you.

The only conspiracy is there is no conspiracy, nobody runs the world, and we're all fucked. Etch that into your tinfoil hat skullcap.

"If you love your country, die for it," he says. I tried, I really did, but *Thundercats* reruns were on TV and I forgot. Too much sugar, maybe. Too little apathy. Too many breaths in lungs of concrete; vape away brothers and sisters, suck on that apocalyptic meat horse substitute, that phony baloney pony. Suck it all away.

Segundo Morris is real, man. I'm not writing these words. He is. He's that shape of a man, that black against black, when you wake up for no reason in the middle of the night, and you stare across your room, and there's that shape, that shade, that needle in your brain that sticks and stabs that won't quite chalk itself up to imagination. He's standing outside your bedroom door. He's standing there right now. Just out of sight. Just around the corner.

Boiled Americans

Case File 005

• Two men, 38 and 46, both typical Americans, were shot at 1:25 a.m. in the 7200 block of South Dobson Avenue in the Grand Crossing neighborhood on the South Side. Both were taken to Stroger Hospital. The younger man was shot in the left leg and right side of his torso, and bullet grazed his head near his left temple. The older man was shot in the upper right thigh. According to poilice, both typical Americans are in stable condition. The older man played chess sometimes in the park with strangers. The younger man smokes a lot of marijuana, but refuses to smoke it in the house, because he is concerned about falling asleep and setting fire to his couch. Both of them once saw a pelican.

VIII. Choose Your Own Fatal Car Accident

[choice 1] If you are an alpha type, a real go-getter, a person of action and agency turn to page 23.

[choice 2] If you are a thinker, a dreamer, passive but deep and careful turn to page 24.

[choice 3] If you are a unique individual, impossible to categorize and innovative turn to page 25.

Boiled Americans

Wake up. Roll over. Check the time on your alarm clock. Get out of bed. Walk to the bathroom. Brush your teeth. Spit into the sink. Apply deodorant. Choice is an illusion. Pick out some clothes. Get dressed. Read the paper. Have some coffee. Greet your pet/significant other/spouse/parent/roommate/probation officer/one-night stand. Find your keys/bike/bus pass. Get into/onto your vehicle. Go to work. Take public transportation if you're particularly eco-conscious/broke/just that way. Feel smug. Choose to choose. You did choose to choose, didn't you? Nobody forced you to choose? Travel. See the world. Quit your job. Be adventurous. Rebel. Fuck the system. Find a new way. Laugh more. Unwrinkle your forehead. Be open to new experiences. Vote. Drink. Eat. Do you think I'm immune? I'm not immune. I do these things too. We share this experience. Free will is real, but that doesn't mean there isn't a script. Have lunch with your co-workers. Move along. Finish your reports. Call your boss. Have a meeting. Sell more merchandise. Pretend you matter. Commute home. Kiss your dog/cat/pet quokka/wife/husband/pastor/congressman/ television. Have some whiskey. Check your websites. Watch a movie. Laugh, and laugh, and laugh, and laugh at people who aren't you. Let the algorithm consume your choices. Let it breathe. Let it gain sentience. It knows you better than you know yourself. I'm not immune to this. It's the same for me. I'm not preaching, I'm sanctified.

[choice 2]

Wake up. Roll over. Check the date on your alarm clock. Get out of bed. Walk to the bathroom. Brush your teeth. Spit into the sink. Apply deodorant. Choice is an illusion. Pick out some clothes. Get dressed. Read the bible. Have some coffee. Greet your pet/significant other/spouse/parent/roommate/probation officer/new god. Find your keys/bike/bus pass. Get into/onto your vehicle. Go to hell. Take public transportation if you're particularly eco-conscious/broke/just that way. Feel smug. Choose to choose. You did choose to choose, didn't you? Nobody forced you to choose? Bullets. See the world. Quit your job. Be adventurous. Rebel. Fuck the system. Find a new way. Scream more. Unwrinkle your forehead. Be open to new experiences. Vote. Drink. Kill. Do you think I'm immune? I'm not immune. I do these things too. There is no immunity. Free will is real, but that doesn't mean there isn't a script. Follow the script to the letter. Move along. Finish your reports. Call your boss. Have a meeting. Sell more weapons-grade plutonium. Pretend you matter. Commute home. Kiss your gerbil/parrot/pet altar boy/wife/husband/arms dealer/editor/brain scanner. Have some tequila. Check your communications. Watch a murder. Laugh, and laugh, and laugh, and laugh at people who aren't you. Let the algorithm consume your ego. Let it breathe. Let it gain sentience. It knows you better than you know yourself. I'm not immune to this. It's the same for me. I'm infected. I'm the worst. I'm the one they warned you about. Weren't you warned? Did they tell you there's no choice? Of course there's a choice. Turn it off.

Boiled Americans

Wake up. Roll over. Check the era on your alarm clock. Get out of bed. Slither to the bathroom. Brush your heart. Spit into the void. Apply deodorant. Choice is an illusion. Pick out some clothes. Get bent. Read the cave paintings. Have some ashes. Greet your slave/nurse/partner/bookie/dealer/governor/dead god. Find your spine/legs/liver. Get into/onto your vehicle. Go to hell. Take way too many prescription drugs if you're particularly eco-conscious/broke/just that way. Feel worse. Choose to choose. You did choose to choose, didn't you? Nobody forced you to choose? Guns. See the universe. Quit your job. Be adventurous. Rebel. Fuck the system. Find a new way. Sleep more. Read the lines in your forehead. Be open to new experiences. Smite. Drink. Forget. Do you think I'm immune? I'm not immune. I do these things too. There is no immunity. Free will is real, but that doesn't mean there isn't a script. Follow the script to the symbol. Move faster. Finish your reports. Call your boss terrible names. Have a murder. Sell more money. Pretend you matter. Blow up your home. Kiss your self/pope/celebrity/bullet/jesus/gun/bomb/Metatron. Have some absinthe. Check your self. Watch a murder. Laugh, and laugh, and laugh, and laugh at people who aren't you. Let the algorithm consume your everything. Let it breathe. Let it gain sentience. It knows you better than you know yourself. I'm not immune to this. It's the same for me. I'm infected. It's too late. Don't you understand? We have the choice. We write the script. But we gouge our eyes with nails sharpened by apathy. I feel it too. Don't let yourself collapse. Fortify your bones. Don't you GET it yet? I'm NOT immune. THERE IS no IMMUNITY. I AM NOT IMMUNE. NOBODY IS IMMUNE.

Now:

☐ Check this box if you don't like following directions.

IX. ▬▬^▬▬^▬▬^▬▬ . . .

earthquakes
lookearthquakeearthquake
earthquakeearthquakeearthquake
it's earthquake weather you can smell it in the air
struck down dumb and tongueless like a galloping corpse
those people were just going to waste their money on dumb things like
food and rent and medical care and insurance and shelter
someone else should take the blame shifting duty
deep underground gas is escaping
until only the smell remains
it stomps you
it steps on your neck parts
you love the pain as the plates shift
those people are others and thus subject to search
enemy androids disguised with masking tape and invisibility
how come all the best songs are about that one dead guy i just made up
there's a woman in bosnia who has three vaginal openings
or is it magic spit that fixes wounds and heals souls
i can never remember what the core
indicates about the weather
but it might rain
it might pour earthquakes
something that only frogs and spiders
are ever supposed to experience in their short lives
which are always shorter when you're hurtling toward ground
at somewhere above sixteen miles per hour depending on your density
as we fall we are judged and stricken and pushed away like a
series of porcupines huddling for warmth in winter
but stabbing each other to death with

warm quills that cause the
ground to shake
it's an eight point two on the
richter scale which tells me one thing
the structures are crumbling in both letter and spirit
the law is a paper target hung up and blowing in the winter wind
frozen solid and burning hot all at once despite warnings from
    weathermen
they have given us all the simple task of predicting earthquakes
so we cut off our ears and throw them to the ground
we watch our blood soak into the earth
we feel the first gentle tremor
we lose ourselves

Boiled Americans

• A typical American in his 20s walked into Mount Sinai Hospital with a gunshot wound to his left hand at 12:45 a.m. He had been shot in the 5500 block of South Lawndale Avenue in the West Elsdon neighborhood on the Southwest Side. His girlfriend is pregnant for the second time. He hopes she decides to keep it. He hates the taste of cilantro. When he was a kid, he couldn't whistle. The wallpaper in his bedroom is a faded blue. He finds it calming.

X. The apes kick the tires, but find they are flat.

Recipe for existential propriety
   (ala ennui)

1 severe dose of media-saturated echolalia
1 stack of books you will never finish
2 cosmic eggs
1 Tsp. dust bunny leavings
8 unfinished tasks, things unsaid
11 guns (various sizes)
1 barrel crude oil
3 parsnips
12 copies of the classic 1946 film *It's a Wonderful Life**

1. Fire up a flu-boiled mind. Heat to 98.6 degrees, depending on altitude, horoscope, and caliber.

2. Mix all dry ingredients like the "great brownie experiment." Hand mixing is preferred and mandatory. Whip into a frenzied dust-devil of a threat.

3. Saute dry mixture in a hot zone. Beware of excess plague monkeys.

4. Cook mixture at 1300 degrees for six hours, basting occasionally with oil based on political affiliations and overall socio-economic level as based on the hidden idea of "class."

5. Pour liquid ingredients over mix, cracking the crust that has developed with a claw hammer to make sure every tiny molecule of your substance is swimming in its own broth.

6. Remove from blast furnace. Your ennui will be in the shape of a broken heart.

7. Cut into chaotic shapes, allow to expand to encompass the greater metropolitan area or the universe at large, whichever is largest at the time of creation.

8. Garnish with parsnips. Serve while molten hot.

I SAID GARNISH WITH PARSNIPS, MOTHERFUCKER.

DO IT.

I . . . I'm sorry. Really. I apologize. That was very much unlike me. I'm not usually that hostile. I am not what you might call a "hostile author." I like my readers. I want to connect with you, and make a fellowship. I am so sorry I blew up about the parsnips. Please, forgive me.

* Note on format: If they are VHS copies, make sure you discard the plastic shells before putting the tape into the mix. If DVD/laserdisc/blu-ray or any other plastic based medium, we recommend you microwave the disc for at least 3minutes on high, then absorb the fractal patterns that appear through the smoke into your skin. Do not use a digital** copy.

** Note on digital copies: The unauthorized reproduction or distribution of this copyrighted work is illegal. Criminal copyright infringement is investigated by federal law enforcement agencies and is punishable by up to 5 years in prison and a fine of $250,000.

This becomes the methodology by which you "break your fast." Sit outside on your break, in the air of bullets, breathing in the casings.

Michael Allen Rose

Luncheon time comes and another meal is chowed down upon. The Woman's Personal Hygiene guide recommends care, to avoid displacement of the pelvic organs. Later on, when business hours are over, we rush back home through crowded streets, stations or subways, fairly jammed with victims, pushing, shoving, elbowing, shooting each other, until one's nerves are so on edge that by the time we get home there is no desire for food.

The digestive apparatus becomes upset and away goes all the fun we thought we had the night before. CONSTIPATION is almost invariably the result. What are we going to do about it? Something has to be done, and quickly; *because a constipated person is an inefficient person.*

Bowel obstructions will continue until morale improves.

Boiled Americans

Case File 007

• Two teens were shot at 12:40 a.m. on the 9600 block of South Carpenter Street in the Longwood Manor neighborhood on the Far South Side. Someone in a light-colored sedan opened fire on the two typical Americans while they were standing outside, the Metatron said. A 16-year-old boy was taken to Little Company of Mary Hospital with a gunshot wound to his left leg and a 19-year-old man was taken to Advocates for Jesuses KKKhrist Medical Center Ala Mode with a wound to the right side of his torso. The older victim was going to ask his boss for this coming Thursday off work so he could renew his plates at the DMV. The younger victim was hoping his mom wouldn't make him get a job this summer. He stole a candy bar and some jerky from a convenience store on his birthday this past year, and laughed about it, but actually felt kind of bad.

*[Memorandum: Angel Number 22 is made up of the number 2 appearing twice, amplifying its attributes. Number 2 relates to your **Divine life purpose and soul mission**, and the Angel Number 22 encourages you to work diligently on your spiritual life path and **soul purpose**.]*

XI. In Remembrance of Forgetting

Stories have an extremely short shelf life. Don't stock your fallout shelter with headlines. They go bad real fast. Collect a bag of cultural detritus and see how fast people forget what's inside. We've already forgotten Columbine. We've already forgotten Ferguson.[8] We've already forgotten Benghazi. We've already forgotten Iraq. We've already forgotten Aurora. We've already forgotten 9/11. We've already forgotten the London subway. We've already forgotten the Boston Marathon. We've already forgotten beheadings in the Middle East. We've already forgotten the Crusades. We've already forgotten ebola outbreaks.[9] We've already forgotten Baltimore. We've already forgotten the faces of our fathers. We've already forgotten our teenage years, birthing pustules from beneath our skin, growing exciting new hair in interesting places, learning to think outside the box of ourselves, voices cracking like liquid lightning, oozing through porous cloth and spatter-painting a tapestry of what we are to become.

   If Billy has ten black people, and nine of them are beaten by cops,

[8] Immediately after the verdict was publicized, there were already reports that major media outlets had published the results of the grand jury's deliberation minutes before it was announced. To many, this was evidence of conspiracy and a media controlled by shadowy figures from behind the government veil. To others, this was another in a long line of tactics being utilized to start a race war. To most, this was evidence of a long standing journalistic tactic of printing up two different stories whenever a major event could only result in one of two binary choices. Much like the infamous incident in which POTUS Harry S. Truman was photographed holding up a major metropolitan newspaper with the headline "Dewey Defeats Truman" on it while celebrating his victory; this was yet another incident in which a tone deaf media was simply hedging its bets in order to scoop competitors and make more money. The press received the news before the public. That is the only reason anyone knows about the verdict at all. There doesn't need to be a conspiracy in place to keep people from getting information when it is all coming from the same sources. Remember that people were misguided by every source from all sides of the political spectrum. The bottom line is, there was no trial. If a crime has been committed, a trial was the preferred methodology for investigating the truth of a situation in the late American century.

[9] If you are an American citizen, you are three times more likely to have married a Kardashian than to contract ebola. You are much more likely to be swallowed whole by a whale than you are to die from ebola. Stay away from the shoreline during mating season (whale or Kardashian) and you will be fine.

34

how many unarmed black people does it take to screw in the light bulb at the tippy-top of the Statue of Liberty torch?

Trick question: It's on fire. Everything is on fire at all times.

Dress yourself up like a comic book character. Feel the revulsion of your fellow man. Now load that rifle with just one more round and see what bit of alchemy you can catalyse. Shoot em' up. Knock em' down. Win a prize if you hit them all.

Hold for the next scandal in three . . . two . . . one . . .

Semen stains glow in the dark. Blood stains don't. That means cum is superior. Or at least, it's evidence you can see during an all-night glow-in-the-dark bowling experience. Spray it everywhere. On the interns. On the victims. On the schoolchildren with their Dora the Exploder back-packs filled with nitro. Put out the international fire with raw human sexuality.

[**PARADIGM SHIFT**]

BUT THAT'S ENOUGH "doom" and "gloom!" There are already too many "metaphors" in this "story" for polite society! Let's have some fun! What shall we do?

I know, I know, says little Billy. We could put on a play!

I can make the costumes! says Peggy Jean.

My uncle has a shed we can use for a playhouse, says Margo.

We can all be in it, and put it on for the neighborhood kids!

You. Reader. You are not dressed for the theatre. No, you are entirely too casual and mundane. Go now, change clothes. Change into something more suitable for the theatre. The book will remain here, simmering away. I promise not to let it run over. I promise. I will wait here.

· · ·

Are you done? If you did not do the thing I just asked you, you are a bad reader. You probably have a poor understanding of allegory, and have probably also forgotten how to make a capital $ when writing in your notebooks.

CHANGE YOUR CLOTHES.[10]*BE THE CHANGE YOU WANT TO SEE IN THE WORLD.*

Now, slip into something more uncomfortable, and find someone to act as a chair [**human furniture fetish version 2.0**] so you can *LEARN ABOUT HOW TO LIVE FROM THE ARTS*:

Begin learning now. (Time yourself! See if you can beat your own record for not giving a shit!)

---

[10] Do not mix fabrics of two different types. See also: The Book of Leviticus.

XII. No Pity: Boiled Edition

JILL GOODACRE is a young girl in training to be a proper lady under the auspices of Renda Liverpool for purposes of citizenship and societal benefit.

RENDA LIVERPOOL is headmistress of an indeterminate place and of an indeterminate age, a proper and good citizen, complacent in society, cruel in interpersonal relationships with her protégés.

The scene is a place not unlike America, a small room reminiscent of a little girl's room, though with all the charm of a cold war brainwashing facility.

The time is midtwentieth Joe McCarthy era century by way of the beginning of the twenty-first century Bush dynasty as filtered through a post nine-eleven world via Obamacare and the future tea party nation under jesus all the way up to and including the reign of our cyber-ape emperor "Bananas the Overmind" and his galley of android slave units.[11] It is also right now.

---

[11] It is fundamentally wrong to assume that because the government official in charge looks like you, they have your best interests at heart. A black president does not mean that he will be a civil rights leader. A female president does not mean advancement for feminist causes and equality. A gay president does not mean that the struggle for equal rights for homosexuals is complete. These people who are elected are not your friends, your allies, your activist heroes. They cannot be. They cannot be both of the system and rebel against that same system. Any politician that you have heard of on a national level in any meaningful way is already so much a part of the system that they are unable and unwilling to commit political suicide to help you. That is the only reason you've heard of them at all. It is foolish to expect anything more, as what you want would be tantamount to a total systemic rejection of the very system that props these people up and sustains them. It is also naive to pretend that fighting the system or trying to change it will be easy or even something that can be accomplished during our lifetime. We have built it to reward people for playing by the rules even as they shout those same rules down and defy their very nature. Revolution in the streets means nothing to the people who are being rewarded by stagnation and an unchanging set of rules. Do not mistake the person for whom you voted for your friend. That mistake will lead to a lifetime of depression and inefficacy. It is true that all lives matter. But the opinion that they matter does not.

Boiled Americans

SETTING: A small room, reminiscent of that of a young girl. Propaganda and Miss Manners posters watch over the room. A sign hangs on the back wall reading: "The Beatings Will Continue Until Morale Improves." The sign is burned into your retinas. You blink, and the after-image is still there.

AT RISE: JILL GOODACRE is sitting on the floor, staring entranced at her fetish object, a small fiber-optic light. Her eyes widen as she begins a low humming sound. She is completely under the spell of the light, when there is a pounding on the door. JILL remains motionless, her humming growing louder. The pounding again, and JILL begins to rock back and forth, until finally RENDA LIVERPOOL bursts in.

---

[12] This week has been a test at work. I have just taken one (1) Vicodin pill and one (1) shot of Agua De Bolivia. Vicodin is a powerful pain reliever made from a mixture of Acetaminophen and Hydrocodone. I have taken it for my stress headache, which was caused by work. Agua De Bolivia is a powerful liquor distilled from the leaves of the South American coca plant, from which the drug cocaine is derived. I have taken it for my stress headache, which was caused by work. This seems like a worthwhile experiment. The combination of these products in my bloodstream might exponentially emphasize one another's side effects, or they might do nothing at all. I have taken one pill and one shot. This is what is called moderation.

The reason that this week has been tough at work is because the company I work for was subjected to an audit, which is a test for companies who work within certain guidelines to see if they are compliant with those guidelines. Part of my job is to specifically make certain that our company is compliant with those guidelines that affect us. At some point in recent months, I let some serious violations of those guidelines slip by my watch, thus creating a situation where my boss had to give me what is known as a written counseling session. Having experienced it, I do not feel particularly counseled. I am, however, acutely aware of my part in the aftermath of the violations, and have been doing everything in my power to fix it. Fixing things is hard. Fixing things in corporate America, especially when government agencies are also involved, is exponentially more difficult.

I am old enough to admit that this particular combination of substances smacks of the kind of self-destructive lack of impulse control that I left behind in my teenage years without ever really experiencing most of the practices that bring those impulses to fruition. However, gentle reader, you should know that the amount of each of these substances was taken in a measured and educated way so as to cause only mild side effects and it is very highly unlikely that I will experience anything outside of general stress relief of the aforementioned stress headache. I remember once when I was young and in love with my first serious girlfriend that I did something impulsive as a cry for attention when I was feeling particularly angry and unloved. I took the sterile surgical scalpel from inside the handle of my survival knife and I very carefully carved her name into my leg. I was not a cutter, nor was I suicidal. I was feeling particularly upset with the world, and I was not being given the attention and care that I felt I needed at the time, so I acted impulsively. My penmanship was excellent. The letters were crisp and red and rounded, like a sans-serif version of the Courier font. Perhaps a shaky Arial. I visited her at work and rolled up the leg of my pants to show her what I had done. She became angry and upset with me. It felt good, because now I was getting the attention I needed. Then, it felt kind of bad, because I knew even then that it was a self-centered ploy for attention, and I vowed to not do that again, because it made me feel weird and guilty. I didn't do it again.

Weeks like this at work, and especially days like this at work, make me feel that need.

I want to carve all of your names into my leg with a sterile surgical scalpel.

I want your names written in my flesh. I want your love. I want you to read these words and feel it.

RENDA: Up! Get up! Come on.

JILL: (*Still staring at the light*) I'm busy.

RENDA: Get dressed. On your feet. You'll never be a lady with a lazy attitude like this.

JILL: I'm meditating.

RENDA: Meditation is for weak-minded individuals without proper breeding. The kind of people who wear white after Labor Day. Ladies who grow long beards. Now get up and get dressed.

JILL: Why?

RENDA: Because today you are a woman, and today is not the day for backtalk, potty-mouth, or other youthful bullshit—pardon my tongue. Today, my young Jill Goodacre, you finally become a real person. Are you excited?

JILL: No.

RENDA: Well why not? A proper lady is excited when gentlemen come to call.

JILL: Is a gentleman coming to call?

Little Billy presses the go button without permission from the stage manager. The play has started. Little Billy casually rubs himself through his chinos.

Peggy Jean cues light cue 2.

Margo is angry with Little Billy. She scowls at him and whispers into the headset microphone that Little Billy eats boogers. Peggy Jean giggles at this.

Light cue 3

RENDA: You know most certainly well that Mister Wrench is coming today to confer your medal of adulthood. Now get up. You don't want him to see you in your pajamas, do you? Nobody gets medals in their pajamas. Don't be vulgar when important gentlemen are coming.

JILL: Mister Wrench is not a gentleman.

RENDA: Nonsense. Children don't know anything about anything. You're being foolish and silly, and little girls who are foolish and silly become sterile and frigid.

JILL: That's not so.

RENDA: Don't back talk me. Make your bed.

JILL: I don't have a bed. You never gave me a bed.

RENDA: Well then tidy your things.

(*JILL walks to her light and moves it carefully once, then looks at it, and moves it back to where it was. She thinks about this, and then moves it one more time: perfect. JILL then walks to the corner and picks up a metal*

Light cue 4. Little Billy refuses to push the button because Peggy Jean refused to give him a blow job back stage when he asked earlier. Margo considers this very petty, and pushes the button herself.

lizard toy. She forgets herself, stroking it for a moment. RENDA makes a guttural noise and JILL quickly places the lizard in its proper place. She finishes tidying up during these last lines.)

JILL: May I go to the bathroom?

RENDA: If you must. First, get the book. You know the drill.

(JILL takes out a large book and brings it to RENDA, who waits, staring holes.)

RENDA: Well, go ahead, dear. We work while we attend to our personal needs, yes? Always be building a better self.

JILL: Yes ma'am.

(JILL puts the book on her head and carefully begins to walk across the room. She makes a false step and the book drops to the floor.)

JILL: Sorry! Please? I really need to go to the bathroom!

RENDA: Ugh. You're like an animal. You know that? Mister Wrench will take one look at you and send you straight to purgatory without supper.

The director, Myron, enters the tech booth, fuming. He wonders aloud whether his crew is trying to wreck the entirety of civilization. Margo, Peggy Jean and Little Billy all mumble an apology.

Someone in the audience sneezes.

JILL: I can hold it.

RENDA: Very well, then. Let's look over your lessons. Where is your workbook?

The same person sneezes a second time.
Everyone waits for the inevitable third.

JILL: Here, ma'am.

(JILL finds her workbook and gives it to RENDA)

RENDA: Good.

(RENDA forces JILL to kneel. She pulls out a blindfold and masks JILL, covering her with something to numb her senses.)

There it is.

RENDA: Now, begin.

JILL: *(reciting)* A lady need not engage in politics. A proper lady allows for natural change to occur. The path of least resistance is the optimal one.

RENDA: Good, next lesson.

JILL: A lady need not make decisions. A proper lady is pretty and delicate, and confuses men so that they might empty their wallets in support of her lavish lifestyle.

Sound cue—traffic. Why? Because.

RENDA: Excellent, you're learning well.

JILL: *(Sliding her blindfold down around her neck)* Why aren't we allowed to do things for ourselves?

RENDA: Please don't ask tiresome questions. You're being bothersome, and it makes me tired, and I want to sleep. If I sleep, I will dream, and if I dream, you will be left without guidance, and you will never become a proper citizen. I am the only one who can turn you into a proper citizen, young lady. If I sleep, you sleep, do you understand?

JILL: No.

RENDA: You're being a nuisance, Jill. Listen to me. In order that our society continue to function, we must make our youth into proper citizens, wouldn't you agree?

JILL: I don't know? I guess. But, who decides—?

RENDA: That is your criminal mind asking questions. Your uterus is filled with terrorists. This reminds one of the lizard brain, and that visceral part of you is no longer welcome here. You're better than a lizard, aren't you, Jill? Come now.

The audience feels sympathetic. A woman in the third row noticeably sniffles. She may have a cold, or she may be extremely emotionally sensitive.

JILL: *(Looking at her toy metal lizard, longingly)* I don't know.

RENDA: Of course you don't know. You're young, dumb and shapely . . . that is, being shaped. By me. You want to be a delightfully witty and charming little capitalist, don't you dear? You want dates to the ball?

JILL: If you say so.

RENDA: Precisely.

(There is a loud knock at the door)

RENDA: You see? I'll bet that's Mister Wrench now. Put on your very best party dress and be ready.

JILL: Renda, wait!

RENDA: What? What did you call me?

JILL: *(fearfully)* Miss Liverpool.

RENDA: We call our betters by their proper names, Jill. How dare you call me by my Christian name. You nasty little creature!

JILL: I'm sorry miss, I'm sorry!

(The knock, again, more

Rolling his eyes, her husband comforts her.

Sound cue—knocking
Light cue 5

Sound cue—knocking
Light cue 7

insistent)

RENDA: You're just lucky that there's someone at the door. Now wash your hands, pick up your sweaters, do the dishes, paint the house, sweep the floors and get a college education. I'll be back shortly with Mister Wrench.

(RENDA exits. JILL sits for a moment, looking around, unsure of what to do. She spies her light and turns it on again, looking lovingly at it. JILL retrieves her toy lizard, and sits before the light, trance and all as before. She begins to speak.)

JILL: Miss Liverpool doesn't know anything, does she, Mister Lizard? Liverpool. Pools of liver. Pool. Loop. Pool. Loop. Loops of liver, livery loops. Liver. Revile. Liver. R, evil. Our evil. Our evil comes out in loops of liver? Evil is the result when you live backwards, Mister Lizard. Who says I have to be a lady? Or a citizen? Why can't I be a canary? Or a trash compactor? Or a sunbeam?

(RENDA enters, looking rather haggard. Her hair is out of place. Her dress is rumpled. Her mouth sits askew on her face in a parody of a smirk. She may have

What happened to light cue 6?

What happened to the audience?

The audience returns from wherever they had been. They are now armed, and audibly cocking rifles and shotguns. This is an odd situation for the theatre club. Little Billy volunteers to see what is the matter.

Little Billy is torn apart by the audience, like a lamb among wolves.

Light cue 8, but having missed 6, we find we are off by one number. The audience begins to shuffle madly. They do not like what Renda is doing to Jill and they are so mad they will not take it anymore.

just been raped. It is difficult to tell.)

RENDA: What are you doing, child? Stop staring at that light. You'll go blind, or get a yeast infection.

JILL: Why don't you like the light, Miss Liverpool?

RENDA: It's bright, dear. It hurts my eyes.

JILL: *(Picking up the light and following RENDA)* But it's just a little light. It chases the darkness away. I sleep with it sometimes.

(RENDA snatches the light away and turns it off)

RENDA: Child, why must you be so difficult? Stop talking about sleep. I don't want to hear of this again. We are going to put this away. I don't like the way you look at it. A lady wouldn't need a silly toy like this.

JILL: Give it back!

RENDA: Do not speak in that tone to me, Miss Goodacre, or I shall boot you in the cunt.

JILL: Where's Mister Wrench?

A man in the front row lights his theatre seat on fire. His girlfriend, or whoever the woman next to him is, grabs the flaming chair and rips it out of the ground, bolts and all, and flings it through the glass of the tech booth. Peggy Jean, Margo and Myron the Director are terrified. They bar the door.

Light cue 9

It does little good. The audience begins to climb in through the broken glass, shouting things like "Where is your God now?" and "This play does not follow the classic Aristotelian model of dramatics!" and "The Patriot Act is yesterday's news! Don't you listen to the drones?"

RENDA: He's twisting his whiskers out in the hall. He's waiting for you to come out and show him how pretty a lady you can be. Where's your dress?

JILL: I don't need a dress. I need my light back.

RENDA: Silly sapling. Stupid fidget. What will people think? They'll think you're no good. A common slut. A porn starlet fresh from the casting couch. No breeding, that's what they'll say. Are you some kind of radical? A leftist? A common hooligan?

(With RENDA paying less attention momentarily, JILL takes her light back, and turns it on. RENDA backs away, scorched. Her skin blackens and falls off into a pile of ashes around her feet. She looks annoyed.)

JILL: My light. It illuminates everything.

RENDA: *(Burning with flames that reach the sky)* I will report all this to Mister Wrench, young lady. I will write it into a report to be published by the administrative office. I will write it in triplicate and distribute it anonymously to internet forums.

Light cue 10. A random audience member, seen chewing on a human femur, presses the button, because he knows the show must go on.

Cue—PYROTECHNICS

(Note: Fire extinguishers have been removed for the duration of the performance, so as not to curtail the effect of the drama.)

Everything is on fire.

Get your dress and be pretty.

JILL: You're not so pretty, yourself, in the light, you know.

RENDA: How dare you speak to me that way. I'll beat you senseless! I'll disenfranchise you!

JILL: *(Holding up the light like a cross to a vampire)* Why are you always lying to me? Why can't I ask you questions, ever? I want to know things. I want to know what's going on outside this room sometimes. I want to know why you make me work so hard to become like you.

RENDA: You are a bad child.

JILL: Why is it bad to question?

RENDA: *(Picking up the lizard, threateningly)* Listen to me, little girl. You will not be brash and coarse and rude. I forbid it.

JILL: Don't hurt him, he didn't do anything wrong!

RENDA: Are we going to behave?

JILL: Put him down!

RENDA: Then let's be a good, sweet girl, and do what you're told. You cannot change the

The theatre is in flames. People are choking all the exit points with their smouldering carcasses. One reviewer writes, "Best experience I've had at the theatre in years!" in his little notebook, just before stabbing a teenager in the eye with a knitting needle and climbing over his body toward an exit.

Cue—Hell

system. It works, it has always worked, and that is that. This is not up for discussion. I make the rules, and you follow the orders. I know what is best for you.

Light cue 11

JILL: What if you don't?

RENDA: I will shoot this toy out of a cannon, straight into Hell. Don't test me, child.

Light cue 12

JILL: No! He doesn't even have a safety helmet!

RENDA: Then put. On. Your. Dress.

(JILL puts the light down, and goes to her dress, which is a rather drab and dull piece of cloth. She puts it on over her pajamas. RENDA lets go of the lizard as she walks to spruce up JILL in motherly, albeit slightly rough ways.)

The few members of the audience still living begin to hum in unison. Something nice. Wholesome.

RENDA: Good. Mission accomplished. Now, don't you feel better?

JILL: Yes'm.

RENDA: That's good. Nice and proper. You look very patriotic. Everyone will be very proud, and you'll look just like all your little friends.

The entire theatre is sinking into the ground. Is there a bog under here? Little Billy's uncle would know, but he's dead now, so it would be difficult to ask. Does anyone have his uncle's phone number?

JILL: I don't have little friends.

RENDA: Yes, you do.

JILL: I've never met them. Will they be there?

RENDA: Of course! You think you're the only one deserving of such accolades?

JILL: I thought so.

RENDA: You're not special, my dear. You're just like the rest. Rows upon rows of perfect little citizens, wearing perfect little uniforms. Marching in perfect unison. It will be perfect.

(JILL begins to roll her sleeves up)

RENDA: What are you doing?

JILL: I'm hot.

RENDA: No, no! A lady never complains, and even if you're hot, you must never show immodesty. People will think you're a whore, or a liberal. You'd be thrown out of the town hall meeting with manners like that. It's a wonder I've been able to teach you anything at all.
(RENDA rolls the sleeves down)

Blood pours from the heating ducts.
The stage hands drown.
The president makes a congratulatory call to the winning team of the Superbowl. Nobody answers, because the whole team was at the theatre. Every team member except the kicker was affected, and they sobbed a lot about their lost freedoms before drowning and burning, as they did.

Now then, look at me.
(RENDA spits on her hand and cleans JILL's cheek of smudges. Her saliva is black and smokes like acid. She is a beast. She is a monster. You see yourself in her eyes. Is it a reflection? It is difficult to tell.)
Very good. One more thing before your test[12]. Miss Goodacre, please recite the pledge.

JILL (mechanically): I pledge to country and to man, to be pleasant as best I can, and every night before I sleep, I'll only sow what I did reap. I will let others run the world, because I am a happy girl, and . . .

RENDA: Go on.

JILL: But . . . it's a lie. I'm not happy.

RENDA: It doesn't matter. You must pretend to be happy, dear. Complacency is a virtue.

JILL: Weren't you ever a little girl, Miss Liverpool? Didn't you want to be something else?

RENDA: Never. I came from the womb just as I am. I knew my place from the beginning.

JILL: Why are things like they

Light cue 395

Cue terrorists.

are, though? Don't you ever wonder?

RENDA: That's the sin inside you talking. The radicalism. You have a terrorist inside you, Jill, and you need to kill him before he takes over.

JILL: But, why?

RENDA: That's the way the machine works. All the cogs in the machine must turn together.
JILL: What if I want to be different?

RENDA: You can't! Nobody changes the system. The blueprint is absolute. You're being a stupid twat, and I won't stand for it. Now give me fifty pushups, recite the national anthem, and find cheaper auto insurance so we can go show Mister Wrench what a good little citizen you are.

JILL: Why do I have to see Mister Wrench?

RENDA: Because you need to grow up and take the place we've made for you in the world.

JILL: *(Holding up the light)* I don't want to see Mister Wrench.

RENDA: Put that down. I will not

Is there anything left alive except for the actors on the stage?

No.

tolerate—

JILL: *(Stalking RENDA, the light out to ward off evil)* You're afraid, aren't you.

Light cue 66829410.5

RENDA: Put on your blindfold. You'll hurt your eyes, and people will spit on you at the street corner and call you a dirty immigrant while you beg for change with a dirty coffee mug.

(JILL takes the dress and throws it at RENDA)

JILL: I'm not going to let you give me any more advice. I'm leaving and I'm not ever coming back into this room.

Everything is gone.

(JILL picks up her lizard and starts to leave)

RENDA: This is unacceptable. There are rules in place!

JILL: I want to make the rules. It's my turn to make the rules.

RENDA: You can't change the law. It's set in stone.

Your freedoms are being eroded.

JILL: I didn't choose them.

RENDA: You don't get a choice.

JILL: I'll take my chances.

(JILL opens the door, and looks out)

RENDA: Be careful, Mister Wrench! She's making trouble! She's a dissident! An enemy combatant!

JILL: They were never my rules.

(JILL sets down the light to block the way, RENDA shrinks from it. JILL takes off the blindfold and throws it down to the ground. She stares down RENDA, then exits. RENDA, cowed, crawls just close enough to the light to retrieve the blindfold, fighting the flames that wreath her as she wriggles closer. She ties the blindfold around her eyes, blinding herself. She rocks back and forth in darkness and bliss, humming a patriotic tune.)
     The lights fade.

The play is over.
Do you hear the machine gun fire?
The audience is dead in their seats, covered in layers of dust, cobwebs, silence. Every man, woman, and child looks as though they have been dead for a very long time. Jawbones have fallen from sallow, sagging cheeks. Moths have eaten holes in the suits and gowns. Concessions have long since rotted and are all infested with larvae.
How long has the play been going on? Was there an intermission? Do you remember?

QUESTIONS FOR CRITICAL THINKING:

Did you enjoy the play? What themes are present?

_____
_____

Where are your little friends? Are you wearing your helmet?

_____
_____

Are flags flammable? Why or why not? Show your work.

_____
_____

Did the television tell you what to do today? Are you listening?

_____
_____

Boiled Americans

```
                \ /
EEEEEEEEEE/L\EEEEEEEEEEEEEEEEEEEEEEEEEEEEEEEEEEEE
EEEEEEEEE/EEI\EEEEEEEEEEEEEEEEEEEEEEEEEEEEEEEEEEE
EEEEEEEEEEEEKEEEEEEEEEEEEEEEEEEEEEEEEEEEEEEEEEEEE
EEEEEEEEEEEEEEEEEEEEEEEEEEEEEEEEEEEEEEEEEEEEEEEEE
EEEEEEEEEEEEEEAEEEEEEEEEEEEEEEEEEEEEEEEEEEEEEEEEE
EEEEEEEEEEEEEEENEEEEEEEEEEEEEEEEEEEEEEEEEEEEEEEEE
EEEEEEEEEEEEEEEESEEEEEEEEEEEEEEEEEEEEEEEEEEEEEEEE
EEEEEEEEEEEEEEEEETEEEEEEEEEEEEEEEEEEEEEEEEEEEEEEE
EEEEEEEEEEEEEEEEEEDEEEEEEEEEEEEEEEEEEEEEEEEEEEEEE
EEEEEEEEEEEEEEEEEEEFEEEEEEEEEEEEEEEEEEEEEEEEEEEEE
EEEEEEEEEEEEEEEEEEEEIEEEEEEEEEEEEEEEEEEEEEEEEEEEE
EEEEEEEEEEEEEEEEEEEEERiEEEEEEEEEEEEEEEEEEEEEEEEEE
EEEEEEEEEEEEEEEEEEEEEEEEEEEEEEEEEEEEEEEEEEEEEEEEE
EEEEEEEEEEEEEEEEEEEEEEEEDEEEEEEEEEEEEEEEEEEEEEEEE
EEEEEEEEEEEEEEEEEEEEEEEEEAEEEEEEEEEEEEEEEEEEEEEEE
EEEEEEEEEEEEEEEEEEEEEEEEEETEEEEEEEEEEEEEEEEEEEEEE
EEEEEEEEEEEEEEEEEEEEEEEEEEE1EEEEEEEEEEEEEEEEEEEEE
EEEEEEEEEEEEEEEEEEEEEEEEEEEEoEEEEEEEEEEEEEEEEEEEE
EEEEEEEEEEEEEEEEEEEEEEEEEEEEEoEEEEEEEEEEEEEEEEEEE
EEEEEEEEEEEEEEEEEEEEEEEEEEEEEEDEEEEEEEEEEEEEEEEEE
EEEEEEEEEEEEEEEEEEEEEEEEEEEEEEEbEEEEEEEEEEEEEEEEE
EEEEEEEEEEEEEEEEEEEEEEEEEEEEEEEEIEEEEEEEEEEEEEEEE
EEEEEEEEEEEEEEEEEEEEEEEEEEEEEEEEETEEEEEEEEEEEEEEE
EEEEEEEEEEEEEEEEEEEEEEEEEEEEEEEEEEPEEEEEEEEEEEEEE
EEEEEEEEEEEEEEEEEEEEEEEEEEEEEEEEEEEEEEEEEEEEEEEEE
EEEEEEEEEEEEEEEEEEEEEEEEEEEEEEEEEEEENEEEEEEEEEEEE
EEEEEEEEEEEEEEEEEEEEEEEEEEEEEEEEEEEEEEEEEEEEEEEEE
EEEEEEEEEEEEEEEEEEEEEEEEEEEEEEEEEEEEEETEEEEEEEEEE
EEEEEEEEEEEEEEEEEEEEEEEEEEEEEEEEEEEEEEERErEEEEEEE
EEEEEEEEEEEEEEEEEEEEEEEEEEEEEEEEEEEEEEEEEAEEEEEEE
EEEEEEEEEEEEEEEEEEEEEEEEEEEEEEEEEEEEEEEEEETEEEEEE
EEEEEEEEEEEEEEEEEEEEEEEEEEEEEEEEEEEEEEEEEEEEEEEEE
EEEEEEEEEEEEEEEEEEEEEEEEEEEEEEEEEEEEEEEEEEEESEEEE
EEEEEEEEEEEEEEEEEEEEEEEEEEEEEEEEEEEEEEEEEEEEEETEE
EEEEEEEEEEEEEEEEEEEEEEEEEEEEEEEEEEEEEEEEEEEEEEEHE
EEEEEEEEEEEEEEEEEEEEEEEEEEEEEEEEEEEEEEEEEEEEEEEEE
EEEEEEEEEEEEEEEEEEEEEEEEEEEEEEEEEEEEEEEEEEEEEEEES
```

Michael Allen Rose

```
EEEEEEEEEEEEEEEEEEEEEEEEEEEEEEEEEEEEEEEEEEEEEEEKEEE
EEEEEEEEEEEEEEEEEEEEEEEEEEEEEEEEEEEEEEEEEEEEEEEUEE
EEEEEEEEEEEEEEEEEEEEEEEEEEEEEEEEEEEEEEEEEEEEEEELE
EEEEEEEEEEEEEEEEEEEEEEEEEEEEEEEEEEEEEEEEEEEEEE\L
                                            / \
```

...and travels even faster

Case File 008

• Three people were shot at 11:20 p.m. Sunday
near the area of 81st Street and Exchange
Avenue—an attack that neighbors described as
a running shootout that left one dead and two
wounded. All three people were typical
Americans. The shooting started with at least
one gunman firing toward two people who had
just walked out of a store at 81st Street and
Exchange Avenue. That shooter wounded two
people—a 25-year-old man and a 19-year-old
woman. The man is in critical condition at
Earthquake Memorial Hospital. He loves to walk
his dog because it gives him a chance to meet
women in the park. He is afraid of deep water
because of the faint memory of a boating
accident when he was a child. The woman was
wounded in the right thigh and taken to
Advocate Christ Medical Center. Her condition
has been stabilized, The Metatron said. She
yelled at her mother on the phone this
morning. She then called her best friend and
talked about it for two hours, ultimately
deciding not to apologize first no matter how
long it took. Her favorite perfume is made
from rose petals and the anal glands of the
North American beaver.[13]
During the gunfire, two others in the
neighborhood started chasing and shooting at

the man, who fled west through a vacant lot while returning fire. During the exchange, a 48-year-old man was wounded in the ankle while on a porch at 80th Street and Escanaba Avenue and taken to Bullet Happiness Hospital in good condition. Police at the scene heard more gunfire after finding the three victims who had been shot and set up a search area three blocks north-to-south and four blocks east-to-west. The man with the wounded ankle watches a lot of reruns of the Richard Dean Anderson vehicle *MacGyver* on television.[14]

Officers from nearby districts responded to the 10-1 call—for an officer in immediate need of assistance—in cars marked and unmarked, with handguns and rifles, in blue uniforms and in green coveralls. According to our sources, the shooting, was unrelated to gunfire from a house on Muskegon Avenue a couple blocks west of the shooting scene. Police found shell casings there but no suspects and nobody was wounded in that round of gunfire. As a helicopter circled overhead, someone shot up a house a couple blocks south on Exchange Avenue, just outside the perimeter police had set up. The gunfire was called over the radio before 911 calls and police ran toward the sound of the gunfire.

The house that had been shot up, in the 8400 block of South Exchange, was near where police responded to a call of a gang disturbance

---

[13] Castoreum is a product derived from the anal castor sacs of the North American beaver. There are twenty-four known compounds in castoreum, some of which involve pheromones. Most often it is described as a vanilla or raspberry in flavor or scent profile. Beavers do not engage in scat porn, however it is likely that if they did, they would be extremely popular.

[14] HOW TO MAKE A BOMB USING ONLY A HANDFUL OF PAPERCLIPS, SOME LAUNDRY DETERGENT, AND AN EGG: [REDACTED]

earlier in the day. A group of gang members had been hanging out outside and someone wanted them removed, The Metatron said. The gang was mostly involved with petty theft and illegal narcotics sales, although several older members were involved in a prostitution ring. One of the gang members had a sister who was two years younger than he was. He loved her very much. For Christmas, he got her a gift card to her favorite seafood restaurant.

XIII. Upload Yourself!

I am become digital. My 8-bit self is surprisingly svelte. Segundo Morris is here. He is a data corruption. The digital afterbirth of a cryptorchid nation.

Avoid him like Evil Otto. Avoid him like Sinistar.**"RUN, COWARD. REAAAAAAAAGGGHH!"** (sic)He is the urban environment's version of a water level.

[DIFFICULTY LEVEL: EXTREME]

How to beat bosses and influence people: On level 3-1, don't jump over the eagle! Instead, jump on his back and use your magic golf club. The wall should open up and he'll fly into the spider web. Once this happens, press up, up, left, left, down and you will fall out of the web, into the pit of pudding. Add the pudding to your inventory and scream into the microphone as soon as the screen turns white. You will see "+2 bonus to semiotics" appear in blue letters at the bottom of the display. (Note: If the letters turn red, quickly unplug your game console and begin praying fervently for salvation.) Look at yourself in the mirror, then find the one missing pixel and smash your screen with a ball-peen hammer. Abuse yourself with a high-grade capsaicin rubdown and smoke some disintegrating airplane parts.

There are power-ups available, if you know where to look. Stars, shrooms, gravity, theoretical particles of ennui.

↑ Up
↑ Up
↓ Down
↓ Down
← Left
→ Right

← Left
→ Right
B
A
Start.[15]

Beep boop beep, but: You're not special. You think you're special, but you only get one life. There are no second chances. If the alien eats you, you're food. If the screen scrolls past you, you're a forgotten fragment of memory. If the bullets hit you, you're a target.

Grab the laser[16]. Use your laser-like incisive wit to cut deep into the heart of the matter. Slice away fatty tissue layers, stone-cold rhetorical boulders become rubble in the wake of your privilege of butchery.Grab the spread gun[17]. Spread your ideas and ideals, you're preaching to the choir boys now, hombre. A fan of five projectile celebrity stars, jutting through paper thin opinionated armor brand hot-dog water.Grab the machine gun[18]. Salt and pepper the devoured class. Eat their weakness for your own.

Remember, if you die, if your avatar becomes part of the eternal static, you default back to your original mode of existential crisis.Grab the fire gun[19]. There's no smoke without a fire. Watch the circles become

---

[15] Thirty lives or not, the most difficult thing about playing Contra was always the second level when you were playing with a friend. Lance (Player one) and Biff (Player two) would start on equal footing, working on the same team against the alien menace. Much like in life, however, if one outpaced the other and leaped too far up the platforms studding the vertically scrolling level, the player on the lower half of the screen would die. There was no saving grace. It was even possible to repeatedly die because the spawn point was manipulated in such a way that the player would reappear over a gap that was impossible to negotiate. Even with many, many chances to live again, death came swiftly and always at the hands of a friend who was too eager for progression.

[16] It looks like an L with wings.

[17] It looks like an S with wings, but kind of slutty. Like it's trying too hard.

[18] It looks like an M with wings. Nobody can figure out why they bothered with a rapid-fire power-up though. The machine gun is basically the rapid fire power-up only without the difficulty of constantly pressing the button until your thumbs ache.

[19] It looks like an F with wings. Fire shouldn't travel in circles, and yet somehow, it does. This power-up breaks physics. Of course, then, so does the concept of death upon falling out of view off the bottom of the screen if your friend jumps too high. What world is this taking place in? The crime problem in major urban areas would look very different with the fire gun. 360 degrees of confusing death each time the trigger is pulled.

concentric. Defy the laws of physics like they were never there in the first place.

It's time for a boss battle.It's time to fight the alien yeti communist vampire foreigner ghost ex-paramilitary feminist homosexual fascist zombie cosplayer.

Pro Tip: Don t shoot pop superstars.

When you get to the final boss, you'll see the final alien overlord! It's a giant, pulsating brain with bright red bulges and thick yellow veins pulsing with lightning flashes! It has two huge eyeballs that have their own lids that envelop them so they can close. You can only shoot the giant brain in the eyes when they're open! The lids are made of some material stronger than titanium! The brain laughs in a really deep, scary voice, even though there's no visible mouth or anus or anything else that the brain could make sounds out of, but then, even though there are no holes for them to emerge from, there are tons of glowing bullets! Glowing, flashing amber bullets fly all over the place in one of three patterns, and if any of them touch you, even the really slow ones that follow a curved trajectory, you will die!

Pro Tip: Always hope to find the crashed airplane in the last place you look.

But, if you can shoot the giant brain in the eyes enough times, it will crack in half! Then, somehow, the brain survives, even though it has been cracked in half, because there's a man inside the brain. He is tall, and green, and he has long hair and some kind of uniform with epilates on it, like he is a ranking member of the military. He will laugh at you and he will push fleshy buttons inside the brain, where he is seated on a golden throne. Then, more bullets will come out of the parts of the brain that are broken, and he will shoot lightning from his hands at you, and if the lightning hits you, you will die! But then, if you shoot him in the face enough times, he will explode in a big ball of fire and blood, and then you will be able to walk through the area of the brain called the medulla oblongata, where the brain stem was attached to the fleshy alien walls. There is a little room beyond the brain's rancid carcass, and you can walk in to see what's there.

Pro Tip: Do not go on a shooting spree in your classroom or place of employment.

The choice you make here will affect the end of the game. There's no going back, even if you use your last fairy bottle, even if you walk through the checkpoint three times, even if you back up your game progress to a solid state drive perfectly positioned at the center of the sun, even if you are a technical wizard genius who can emulate a save state in his or her sleep . . .

If you choose the green gem . . . you have decided to join the machine uprising and forget about the time portal. The army will attempt to stop you, however, because you picked up the marmalade robot; they will be unable to affect your rivet shield. Your toenails will grow at a rate of one point two inches per cyber-moment until they fire from your feet in a show of solidarity with the android liberation front. This is canonically considered the "bad ending."

Pro Tip: If your perceived oppression level goes above 50% be sure to invert it.

If you choose the red skull . . . your long suffering spouse will suddenly appear from inside a nearby telephone booth, and shoot you with the gigantism ray. When this happens, all the money you have collected will be converted into pure human blood, which will be used to solidify the nee-ya fuel supply station in the Andromeda Prime system. Your belly button will open to reveal that the pilot worm has been running your thought beams since the party early in the game, just outside of Juarez. This is canonically considered the "bad ending with bacon and chives."

Pro Tip: Do not blow yourself up for The Metatron.

If you choose the violet eagle . . . the system will shut down, leaving you impotent and isolated; however, one single message will come through your combination communication sleeve and girth conversion system. Opening it, you will see that the people of Norway are finally free of the loop chain that has been binding their spirit pelicans to the mundus. They will sail their hero boats out in your honor as the impending horror settles into your hemo-nest. This is canonically considered the "bad ending inverted by whores."

Pro Tip: Stop distracting yourself from what is important.

Or, you could make the choice that nobody wants to talk about. The choice that everyone is afraid to make. Just stop. Stop. Stop it. STOP IT. Quit. Never load the game again. Never put it into the machine that reads the data and converts it into audio-visual data. If you're using physical media, smash, burn, scar, and manipulate it. Break it down into component parts. Smash those parts to atoms, or as close as you can comfortably come with your pathetic human digits. Take those pieces and burn them, scorch them, use the power of microwaves and digital thermometers, and leave nothing but ashes. Take those ashes and eat them. Swallow them, Digest them. Wait, and shit them out. Take the shit and bury it, somewhere far away. Somewhere you've never been. Drink until you can't remember where you are or how to get home, and bury the shit in that place, then walk until you are lost. Wait until you sober up, go home, get into your bed and hide under the covers, trying to forget you ever played it.

That choice is just as legitimate as any other. It means just as much as anything that was programmed for you.

[HACKING INTO DATABASE]

{{press here to begin}}

0100011101100001011011010110010101110010011001110110000101110
1000110010100100000011010010111001100100000011100000110111 1
0110100101101110011101000110000110010101110011011100110010 0
0000110110101101001011100110110110111101100111011110010110110 0111
100100101110[20]

---

[20] Note: Applies only to paper edition of this book. DO NOT ATTEMPT WITH E-BOOK.

Michael Allen Rose

I AM READING YOUR THOUGHTS.

[ENTER AGE]
[ENTER RACE]
[ENTER GENDER]
[ENTER CREED]
[ENTER LEVEL OF PSYCHIC DISCOURSE]
[ENTER PRIVILEGE/HANDICAP]
WARNING: DATA CORRUPTION IN SECTOR 462.6
DO NOT TURN PAGE[OFF] ACCELERATOR 325.666.querty
TAKE THE LORD'S TRUE NAME AS YOUR WI-FI PASSWORD

XIV. Explain, Now.

The police bring in military grade hardware. They are armed with assault rifles, perched atop tanks. On the front of each tank, a gigantic meat-grinder. Complacent people of color are forced to crank the handle as the tank rolls over protesters, turning them into sausages, and why not? Everyone loves sausages. Raise your voice and get turned into a glass of animal juice. Feed the state your head. You are filled with nutrients.

They check your pockets at the door to make sure you're openly carrying a weapon. If you're unarmed, that's a death sentence; that's a subtextual longing for the grim spectre of death to parse your flesh for meaning with a dozen rounds of fifty caliber machine gun bullets. Pull out the copier paper. Does your shade match it? Lucky devil; tear gas for you, drink it down, suck it up, sniff it in, become one with the police state. Remember when our biggest problem was a blow job? I sure could use a blow job right now.

Occupy your cell. Fight the power that makes your morning coffee. Would you like to make a donation today to the policeman's ball? It's actually a ball-gag. We're going to strap you down and blow off rounds all over your face. Catch a bullet, win a shiny nickel. Tear gas inhalers, rubber bullet kisses, a flood of urgency clamoring for your attention. They eat your children.

The media is a headache, shuddering spasms climbing our spinal cords, shaking pieces from our Pangaea and forming new continents of malice. They turn on the hoses and wash us away. We are chalk in a rainstorm. Following the bouncing rubber bullets and sing along to the sirens and epithets. But we are too self-obsessed to finish the song. The story will creep back under the minutiae, burrowing down with the invisible worms until the next time the skulls of children are cracked loudly enough to resonate.

Michael Allen Rose

Case File 009

• A man in his late teens was shot in the leg at 10:10 p.m. at 87th Street and Morgan Avenue. He was hit in the leg and taken to he Rancid Eye of Jesus Medical Center, The Metatron said. The man, a typical American, had a favorite food: tacos. He could eat them every day without getting tired of them. The last time he had a head cold he got very irritable with his friends. He hates fried rice. He eats earthquakes for breakfast.

XV. Genetic decoder rings.

T hese animals are inescapable; these Lebanese barking mountain spiders, these hateful, hopeless won-ton soup masturbators. The right to exist in a sane world coupled with a dual-crested duck-billed platypus of a fucked up future. This elevated status symbol gives green stamps for the war. Safety precautions must vibrate at the correct frequency.

NOTICE TO ALL INVOLVED:
You are now entering the genetic manipulation facility. Please prepare your hard hats, safety vests, rubber boots, safety scissors, hard vests, moon boots, rubber nipples, nipple clamps, and other sundry items.

FIRST FLOOR: Ladies' hats, coat hangers, mason jars, albacore tuna.

SECOND FLOOR: Lawnmowers, tchotchkes, sausage, canned yams.

THIRD FLOOR: Baseball cleats, ennui, rape kits, photocopier supplies—

Ma'am, please keep your limbs inside the ride at all times.

FOURTH FLOOR: Illegible handwriting, ascots, bucket lists, hidden agendas.

SIXTH FLOOR: Harmonicas, winnebagos, tapeworms, animated cartoon shows of the—

Sir, we're speeding up now, no need to be alarmed. No need outside the usual, anyway. Relax, and let the cables do their work.

SEVENTEENTH FLOOR: Robots[21], slot machines, dirty nickels, timeshare presentations.

FIFTY-THIRD FLOOR: Gasoline, credit cards, fruit snacks, fatback.

ONE-HUNDRED AND FORTY-SEVENTH FLOOR: Action, suspense, chills and thrills!

BASEMENT: Everybody off.

We find ourselves standing in a large laboratory. The walls seem to stretch for miles. It reminds me of the warehouse in the Indiana Jones movie where they hide the Ark of the Covenant. I wonder, briefly, if this is the same warehouse, only repurposed.

The tour begins.

The wily goose-billed superhorse. Rare expunged penguins.

A cheetah in sunglasses and a raincoat does an ollie kickflip over our heads and lands in a vat of Mountain Dew. Cannons fire extreme burritos into the air along with purple fireworks. We are in the heart of evolution's silver lined coffin now.

I stare across the room and lock eyes with Segundo Morris. His shadow has grown gills and a prehensile tail from each of its eye sockets. He swims and swings away into nightmare. Meanwhile, I am set before myself with a hammer and many nails of faith, an amoeba learning mitosis by peering through a leak in the omnipresent meaning.

I try joining the Segmented worms over in Annelida, and grow multiple circular segments. I feel like I'm being strangled in a mummy wrap sweater. The Arthropods seem to have it better, with their segmented bodies and jointed limbs. Evolution throws in a free chitin exoskeleton with every purchase. Then I realize that despite the physical protection this offers, I suddenly feel human again. I'm one of over 1,134,000 types, and yet I feel alone at the dance, even surrounded by other members of my television-induced hive mind. I tap my exoskeleton with my reversible spiny proboscis that bears many rows of hooked spines. I am trying to impress others at the dance by pretending I am a thorny-headed worm of the Acanthocephala kind; however, they see through my disguise and the tour continues. Everyone seems to have

---

[21] Two of the smartest men of the twenty-first century, Elon Musk and Stephen Hawking, have both stated that advanced artificial intelligence is the most dangerous existential threat to human existence. Far from the slaves that we assumed they would become when we began programming, robots have advanced to the point now where they are not only capable of doing things that humans do at a superhuman level, but some can re-design themselves to be more efficient and effective at an exponentially increasing rate. The technological singularity is often described as the moment where virtual reality becomes so realistic that we are unable to discern it from our own physical reality. As harrowing as this sounds to humanists (and as utopian as it sounds to technophiles) in all likelihood we will first perfect a computer that can learn and rebuild itself much faster than we are able to stop it. We will all be slaves to the robots, or dead and buried, long before the technological singularity is achieved. Treat your microwave well. Be polite to your toaster. Take your electric milk frother to a baseball game some time. You want to be on the right side when the time comes.

partnered up now except for me and Segundo Morris. I frantically look around for a potential hook up, anything to feel less alone. I cannot approach the beings I see. I am gutless, like the Acoelomorpha, no digestive tract to give me the guts to act. My feet combine themselves into something like a tank-tread and I take on the aspect of the mollusks. I grow umbrella-like scales at each end of the thing I call my torso. I am a corset bearer, a loriciferic mess.

I idly play with my priapulida, sending my little priapus into ecstatic spasms. The Y-chromosomes around me mix and mingle and shake like a martini, unstirred. Zeu's mistress, the phoronida, lends me a U-shaped gut. I feel a tug on my cord as I develop the post-anal tail of a chordate. I fire nematocysts into the ether, and the ether bunny angrily fires back a volley of epithets. Now I will never be loved. Segundo Morris, meanwhile, has developed a spine. My skin is soft, I am no echinoderm. I am a sea mat. I cannot find lungs. My reproductive organs are two cards short of a flush, and none of them match. I look into a conveniently placed mirror that doubles the size of the room, and see myself as a little-ringed, joint-footed, thorny-headed, gut-without, strong-footed, brush-headed, horse-shoe bellied, corded, smooth-skinned invertebrate. The tour guide screams at something underneath us, way below my level of consciousness; he pumps all the ocean out of the room, and suddenly I'm expected to breathe nothing but burning air.

I am indistinguishable from a black-head. I am Flesh Worm. A minute little creature, scientifically called *Demodex folliculorum,* hardly visible to the naked eye, with comparatively large fore body, a more slender hind body and eight little stumpy processes that function as legs. No specialized head is visible, although of course, there is a mouth orifice. I hunger for skin.

I live on the sweat glands or pores of the human face, and owing to the appearance that I give to the infested pores, I am known as a "black-head." I wish to disfigure the otherwise pretty face of our tour guide. Segundo Morris will also be disfigured by ugly creatures such as me. Although we insects are nearly transparent white, the black appearance of the skin is really due to the accumulation of dirt which gets under the edges of the enlarged sweat glands and cannot be removed in the ordinary way by washing, because the abnormal, hardened secretion of the gland itself becomes stained. We insects are so lowly organized that it is almost impossible to satisfactorily deal with us, and we will cause the continual festering of the skin which we inhabit.

I have gotten away with murder. I am more efficient than the bullets that spread my seed to the newspapers. But then . . . the advice: Press them out with a hollow key or with the thumb and fingers, and apply a mixture of sulphur and cream every evening. Wash every morning with the best toilet soap, or wash the face with hot water with a soft flannel at bedtime. I am subjected to the most painful of all expulsions. I am no longer evolving, but devolving. I am headlines. I am media saturation. I implode to a microscopic ink spot and then my memory is a stain.

I wish I had become Ionesco's Rhinoceros. Green, and scaly, and metaphorical.

Kingdom: Animalia
Phylum: Chordata
Class: Mammalia
Order: Perissodactyla
Family: Rhinocerotidae
Genus: Ceratotherium, Dicerorhinus, Diceros, Rhinoceros
Species: *Ceratotherium simum* (White Rhinoceros); *Dicerorhinus sumatrensis* (Sumatran Rhinoceros, Hairy Rhinoceros, or Asian Two-Horned Rhinoceros); *Diceros bicornis* (Black Rhinoceros, Prehensile or hook-lipped rhinoceros); *Rhinoceros sondaicus* (Javan Rhinoceros, Asian lesser one-horned rhinoceros), *Rhinoceros unicornis* (Greater One-Horned Rhinoceros, Indian Rhinoceros)
Subspecies: *C. simum cottoni* (Northern White Rhinoceros, presumed extinct), *C. simum simum* (Southern White Rhinoceros); *D. bicornis michaeli* (Eastern Black Rhinoceros), *D. bicornis minor* (Southern Central Black Rhinoceros), *D. bicornis bicornis* (Southwestern African Black Rhinoceros), *D. bicornis longipes* (Western Black Rhinoceros, declared extinct in 2011)

I would be an allegory for fascism.I would do it without complaint.Presume me extinct.I just want to belong to a "crash" of something.I just want to belong.I just want to crash.I just want to—
DING
And we crash back into the first floor.

Boiled Americans

Case File 010

• At 9:50 p.m. in the 8400 block of South Loomis Boulevard, someone shot two typical Americans. One, 19, was taken to Holy Cross Hospital with a gunshot wound to his arm; his condition was stabilized. The second, 22, was shot in the shoulder and taken to Advocate Under McDonaldland Kazoos Medical Center. She had a small doll collection in one of the spare closets in her apartment. Occasionally, she used ecstasy at a club when she was out dancing, but she generally avoided what she referred to as "white drugs." She was the first person to wish her mother a happy birthday last year. The two of them had known each other for seven years. There were unrequited and complicated romantic feelings from both of them toward the other, but historically, never at the same time.

XV. In Soviet Russia, Joke Tells You

I was walking home from the bread line when I tripped over a metaphor and walked into a door. It was an old metal door, the kind from back alleys of the nineteen-thirties where rum was delivered to the back of speakeasies by gangsters and children and urchins. I knocked on the door, and a notch slid open at eye level. Two dust bunnies peered out at me, coated in pepper and shame. I asked to speak to their manager. They told me that he wasn't in, that he'd died, that his clock had stopped ticking, that his plums had shriveled into prunes, that his danish had gone stale, that his veins were popping with heroin needles and lichen, that his broken flag was jammed halfway up the windpipe and the hills were alive with the sound of choking.

"I ran into your door," I said. "It was there one minute, and then it wasn't, or vice-versa," I contradicted myself. The indictment was set for next Thursday at seven. I put it in my calendar, which is the head of a pin underneath the alarm clock.

The dust bunnies regarded me, and my lack of a conspicuous flag pin on my lapels, and in fact my lack of lapels altogether, and replied in a voice like wet thunder: "You got bird insurance?"

I assured him, most assuredly, that I did not. "No, I do not," I said.

We both looked down at my shoes, covered, cemented, besmirched with bird excretions. "Got to have bird insurance. It's the law. How else you gonna' feed your family, papa bear?"

I tore open my chest and handed him a kidney. He sneered at it like a kid on the bus with rickets. I spat and the world groaned. "Come on, pally," I said, "be a friend and give me a breakfast. I ain't got no charity to speak on, and no soap box under my footfalls."

It was obvious he didn't care. He shoved bird insurance forms in triplicate out the slot, and I ate them up like pac-man, *wokka wokka*

Boiled Americans

wokka. I shit carbon copies for three days. At the end of the third day, I stood up, gathered my druthers, and re-knocked, capitulating to the circumstances of whimsy that led me to crash headlong into this mess firstwise.

The slot was gone, and in its place, a muffin. I didn't have muffin insurance either, and I didn't want to take my chances.

Michael Allen Rose

Case File 011

• At 8:20 p.m. Sunday, a 29-year-old man was shot at 101st Street and Emerald Avenue in the Roseland neighborhood on the Far South Side. He was taken to Diddly-Hoo-Ha-Ha-Hospital to be treated for his wounds. He was a typical American. He was obsessed with editing his photos before he would allow them to be posted online because of a small facial scar. He saw it every time he looked in the mirror, but most people didn't notice it at all until he pointed it out. He fell on a rake when he was a kid, and was very self-conscious about it. He liked to imagine being a space adventurer superhero of some kind, but ultimately knew deep down that he didn't have the conviction to really make a go of it.

XVI. The First Cause—The Unmoved mover

Praxis: To *do* something.

Ethos. Your rationality. An invisible essence drives the universe, pushing to make things what they should be; social forces drive us or draw us toward the action. Now do. Go out and commit to something. Slacktivism causes cancer. Break out of your self-inflicted gunshot wound conspiracy and act.

Poesis: To *make* something.

Pathos. A passion. We yearn to reach. We strive to become what we can become. Create. Fold this book into a pair of three-dee binocular opera glasses. Make some soup, and feed it to your ego. Leave a lasting impression that isn't simply an impact crater or the bio-spawn of your friendly neighborhood germ cells.

Theoria: To *think* something.

Logos. The logic. True pleasure emerges from becoming the ultimate expression of what we are. Consume and regurgitate. Figure out all the angles, then take the shot. Be religious, not for Jehovah but for Jumpin' Jiminy Christmas.

DO NOT COMPUTE.

KEEP FIT TO FIGHT.

This is a man-to-man talk, straight from the shoulder without gloves. It calls a spade a spade without camouflage. Read it because you are a soldier of the United States. Read it because you are loyal to the flag and because you want the respect and love of your comrades and those you have left at home.

HEALTH WILL DO MUCH TO WIN THE WAR.

Next to military obedience there is nothing so important in a soldier's life as health, and if he practices military obedience, as every true soldier must, he will surely have good health.

Your health is even more important than ammunition. Without health, ammunition is worthless.

Your health is even more important than guns. Without health, guns cannot be effectively manned.

Your health is even more important than bravery. Bravery in bed does not win battles.

Your health is even more important than efficient officers. Without healthy soldiers, the greatest officer is helpless.

Diseases kill more soldiers than bullets, but such diseases as smallpox, yellow fever and typhoid have been practically wiped out. Today the greatest menace to the vitality and fighting vigor of any army is venereal diseases (clap and syphilis). The escape from this danger is up to the patriotism and good sense of soldiers like yourself.

Will-power is the first preventative when temptation comes. If you and your comrades use the "I'll-be-damned-if-I-do" will-power against sexual desire, venereal diseases in the army will be conquered and there will be much less to fear from the enemy.

Will-power and courage go together. A venereal disease contracted after deliberate exposure through intercourse with a prostitute is as much of a disgrace as showing the white feather.

A soldier in the hospital with venereal disease is a slacker.

He keeps equipment idle.

He keeps a uniform out of service.

He leaves a break in the line.

He must have the attendance needed by men disabled in the honorable discharge of duty.

His medicine and care cost money that could be otherwise used to win the war.

He has lost self-respect, which is the backbone of every true soldier.

If you go with a prostitute, you endanger your country because you risk your health, and perhaps your life. You lessen the man-power of your company and throw extra burdens on your comrades. You are a moral shirker.

WOMEN WHO SOLICIT SOLDIERS FOR IMMORAL PURPOSES ARE USUALLY DISEASE SPREADERS AND FRIENDS OF THE ENEMY.

Boiled Americans

No matter how thirsty or hungry you were, you wouldn't eat or drink anything that you knew in advance would weaken your vitality, poison your blood, cripple your limbs, rot your flesh, blind you, and destroy your brain. Then why take the same chance with a prostitute?

Hark! A counterpoint!

HEALTH is to BEAUTY as the VINE is to the GRAPE. Beautiful, luscious grapes do not grow on sickly stems. They grow on vines which are well-cared for and free from vermin and disease.

POSTURE also plays an extremely important role in the maintenance of good health, attractiveness and PERSONALITY.

The branks will help develop your personality. Put the cage over your head and bite down on the scold's bridle.

Pull in the abdominal muscles, thrust the hip bones forward and put the weight on the balls of your feet. The shoulders will take care of themselves.

Long neglected saggy facial muscles, wrinkles, double-chin, etc. may be helped only through the medium of surgery.

I spent an hour at the roller rink once after falling face first onto a concrete floor. My top row of teeth had gone through my bottom lip. I left a trail of bloody handprints all the way to the bathroom. I didn't call my parents for an hour because I was there with girls.

I conducted myself with honor and trembling, bloody hands.

Now someone else needs to catch a bullet. Our next victim is:

Michael Allen Rose

Case File 012

• A 30-year-old typical American man was shot about 8:45 p.m. Sunday at 66th Street and Hoyne Avenue. He was taken to Advocate for Bacon Medical Center with wounds to the left side of his back. He had a tattoo of a cross on his left arm, done in a gilded, antiquated sort of style that his tattoo artist had referred to as "old world." Though no longer a Christian himself, he considered his ties to the faith he grew up in important enough to permanently scar his skin as a nostalgic remembrance of his childhood. If you asked him, he would tell you that for him, its meaning was "strength." He had been in numerous fights, but proudly talked about the fact that he didn't carry a gun.

XVII. Evil Moving Pictures

I find myself at a wrap party with Segundo Morris. Everyone is having a great time. We are Hollywood's elite. We are the beautiful people.

I have been working on a feature length film for four weeks. This was my first time working as a crew head. I am the majority of the art department. I was responsible for setting all the props in each location and making sure that the physical reality of the space was accurate and consistent from shot to shot.

Everyone is drinking from a punch bowl at the center of the room. The punch is green, smoking, clouds of what appears to be corrosive gas rolling from inside the rim and down onto the floor, where it dissipates into vaporous nothing.

Michael Allen Rose

The room looks like this:

```
     ooo0OOO                        ooo0OOO
   ooO    ooO                     ooO    ooO
  oO         oO                  oO         oO
  oO  pickle chips  oO           oO  potato skins  oO
  oO         oO                  oO         oO
   ooO    ooO                     ooO    ooO
     oooo0OO                        oooo0OO


                      reasons
                  to incite random
     ooo0OOO      moments of violence        ooo0OOO
   ooO    ooO    drink the delicious punch  ooO    ooO
  oO         oO   change the channel but   oO         oO
  oO  veggie tray  oO  nothing is on kill your  oO  fried cheese  oO
  oO         oO      television brain      oO         oO
   ooO    ooO           silence             ooO    ooO
     oooo0OO                                  oooo0OO


                     ooo0OOO
                   ooO    ooO
                  oO         oO
                  oO  shroom caps  oO
                  oO         oO
                   ooO    ooO
                     oooo0OO
```

Boiled Americans

I reach over and grab a deep fried pickle off the silver tray. This is a classy affair: they have made them from pickle chips instead of pickle spears.[22] I bite down and let the piping hot brine trickle over my tongue.

The lights dim, and a single spotlight illuminates the man who started all this. He is a writer, producer, director and actor, and might have even been responsible for the craft services. I am not sure.

"We worked hard, and it paid off, and now we have made this product," he says as a screen lowers from the ceiling behind him. "Our shared vision has begat this piece of celluloid communication that we shall transmit to the world." I wish I had some popcorn, but popcorn is not available at this particular time. "As a special surprise, you are all invited to the premiere of the film, which will happen right now in this very space." They must have worked very hard to complete a cut of the movie in the very short amount of time that has passed since we stopped shooting only hours ago.

The spotlight dims and the screen blazes to life.

I'm watching the movie, but I find that I'm unable to remember any of the scenes that are shown. I was there for every single shoot, ninety-five percent of the time, maybe more, and yet there are no shots in this movie that I remember, nothing occurring here that I worked on.

What have I been doing these past four weeks?

I rub my shoulders, still sunburnt from spending an entire day of shooting outdoors in blazing one-hundred degree sunny weather without any sunscreen. I blistered and popped, red like a cherry, still aching underneath my shirt. There are no scenes taking place in the bright sunlight in the movie. Every single scene that is not indoors either takes place in the evening or during a rainstorm.

There is a scene with a casino, where people are gambling. I see myself as an extra in the background, while the shot pans across the casino floor. It couldn't have been me, because I was never in the shot, and was not an actor in the film, but before that background character slid off screen I am certain it was me.

There is a scene around a campfire, where the characters are talking to a mysterious man they met in the woods. They fall asleep around the campfire, and when they awaken in the morning, the old mysterious man is no longer there. I do not remember seeing the man, and I do not remember making the camp fire, which would have been part of my duties. Where have I been for the past four weeks?

---

[22] Pickle spears often slip out of their deep-fried casing when bitten, which can cause hypercube scorching of the face and genitals.

Now, the room appears like this:

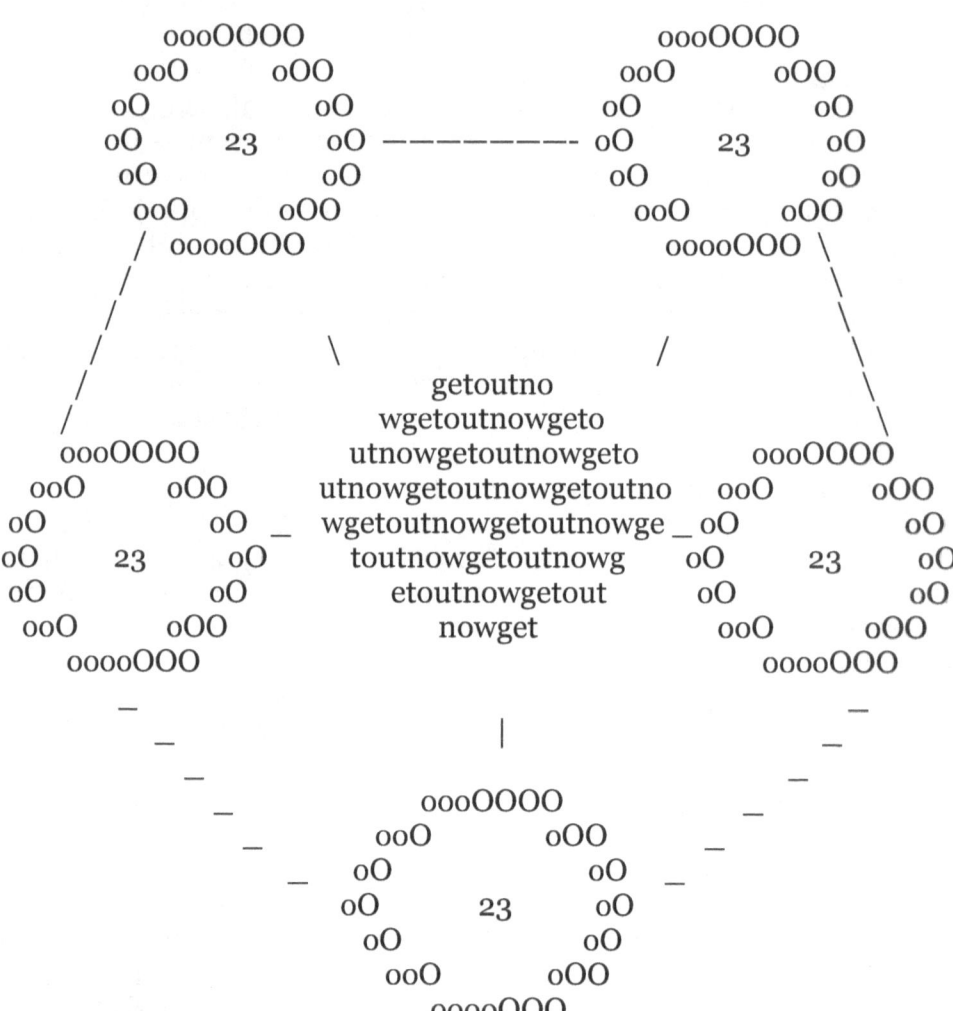

Boiled Americans

My paycheck is in the envelope I'm holding so I find a dark shadow to stand in and unseal it, but when I open it, flies pour out instead. Two of the bigger ones fly off with my pickle spear. I am hungry, and confused, and the movie is still running.

Now there's a suburban home on the screen, and the characters are pulling stockings over their heads, and checking their firearms. They are about to rob this house. I do not remember seeing anything like this in the script, but I remember that I was there for every single shot. The movie was about a group of friends meeting a wise old man while camping just a minute ago, and now they are about to break into and enter a suburban home. I squint at the screen and realize that they are standing on the back porch of the house that I grew up in; the house my parents live in. No lights are on in the house. Didn't my parents move to a different house after I moved out? I was sure they did, but this is the house I grew up in. There's the fence in the background that marked the edge of our lawn. There's the crack in the corner post of the porch where I ran into it with the riding lawnmower one hot summer.

I look down again and all the food is gone. Every exit from the room is blocked. I could try to squeeze through the crowd; my fellow crew members would surely part to allow me to pass through, but I don't recognize anyone here. Where have I been for the past four weeks? Who are these people, laughing and clinking champagne glasses together?

The film is now showing all the members of my family as well as the protagonists sitting down at my parents' dining table for a turkey dinner. My father is carving the turkey. My mother is passing mashed potatoes to the "funny fat character" of the group. He gets some on his nose while trying to balance the bowl in one hand and the serving spoon in the other.

I can't help but wonder why I wasn't invited.

I think hard about the college dorm scenes. The friends in the film are in college, and hang out together in a college dorm room. I dressed the set myself, using old posters and ephemera from my own college days. There was a psychedelic beanbag chair that the main characters took turns sitting in. When the dorm room scene comes along, there is no furniture in the room. They all stand awkwardly. There is very little dialogue in the scene, with short awkward small talk punctuating long periods of silence. Occasionally, someone coughs, and all the characters look around awkwardly, like they don't know what to say or do next. The camera lingers on them for a very long time. I wonder what happened to my family. I should call my mother more often.

Suddenly, it's a crime procedural.

A case file appears on the screen. Everyone turns and looks at me. Everything thinks I know what to do. I am petrified.

Boiled Americans

Case File 013

• At 6:28 pm., a 21-year-old man suffered a wound to the knee in the 1500 block of North Mason Avenue in the North Austin neighborhood on the West Side. He was in good condition at Loretto Hospital and one person has been arrested, The Metatron said. He was a typical American. He had been sitting around outside with his friends before the incident, talking about putting together a new mixtape and freestyling, trying to get a demo into a hands of a hip-hop producer. This had been his dream since he could remember. Once, he sold a demo CD to a white man on the subway, who had convinced him that he was connected to the music industry. The white man actually worked as a sound guy at a dive bar that hosted bands every weekend and didn't pay—

NO. NOPE. IT ENDS NOW.

CASE FILE 1001010110100101:

The TYPICAL AMERICAN EDITOR of the major metropolitan newspaper from which the information in these case studies was taken insists on capitalizing words like "Far" in the context of geography. He or she also appears to be obsessed with "approximate times" of shootings. There is something interesting about how the word "FAR" is capitalized and emphasized. It speaks to the cultural "othering" that white north-siders tend to do when they talk about where the violence happens. It doesn't happen in OUR neighborhood, they capitalize. It happens FAR away on the South/West/Other side. "Far South Side" sounds much further away from the gentrified neighborhoods on the north side, which apparently does not need to be capitalized because it is simply a direction where the neighborhoods are less filled with bullets and people of color. The TYPICAL AMERICAN EDITOR has been executed. Editorial duties will now be outsourced. Case studies should be far more inclusive from here on out. We apologize for any inconvenience.

Now that we've taken care of that, let's continue on with politics for a bit. Everything is political, even when it isn't. That's why I'm moving in a new direction.

XVIII. Consortium Imperii

I'm trying to bring back the Whigs. I want King George off my turnip farm.

The ship arrives. It drops anchor. The gangplank is lowered. A shuffling mob of treasonous jackanapes rat-tat-tats off the ship, clicking heels through headspace and keening like a mob of banshees.

A royal chair is introduced. Not quite a throne. Not quite a bent over serf. A chair. But it's royal. I can tell in the same way that you can tell in a dream that you're in your grandpa's house, eating bowl after bowl of your grandma's potato chowder, even though from the look of things you're actually in a hut in the middle of the Serengeti and nothing is getting any easier because every time you pick up the spoon, more teeth fall out.

The King sits.

"Farumph. Hear ye, hear ye."

Spearmen rappel down from the rafters, forcing us at the point of their nomenclature to drop to our knees and bow until our heads touch the inmost light. The wood is hard and unforgiving. I feel my patella pop, cracks of discomfort spreading through me like movie-theatre butter-flavored synthetic coconut oil.

"Those of you who look to me as more than a king, perchance some kind of demigod or emperor, please remain supplicated. The rest of you may leave."

Half of us stand, and are immediately pushed through the doors into a large meat-grinder. I know that the sausages will go into the soup. I salivate uncomfortably. The buzz of the machine makes my taste buds stand up and salute. We, the ones still kneeling before our lord and slaver, look up and await further instigation.

"Please stand if you believe that I, as your emperor, have no clothes."

All but three of us stand. I look, hesitating, at his majesty, wondering why I see him in a three-piece ape suit and a tutu in full clown makeup. I voted for him. I would still dangle my chad for this magistrate.

The group is shuffled off to Buffalo, as the vaudevillians would sing. Buffalo, in this particular instance, is an allegorical city, one filled with razor sharp knives made of alligator bear wolves with bad attitudes and very little to say about anything pleasant. These people, all but the three of us remaining, are turned into chopped liver, the kind that is widely ignored in most metaphorical circumstances.

Adjusting my bow tie, I spy a gnat buzzing around the head of the fellow to my left. He immediately unhinges his jaw like a frog who thinks he's a snake and fires a torpedo tongue. A direct hit sinks all hope, and the king wrinkles his forehead in a replicant impulse of disgust. The fly eater is promptly defenestrated repeatedly. As a show of power and theatricality, guards remove the window from the castle wall and send the poor soul through it thirty-seven times. The same window. His epitaph will be ridiculous—the final insult.

A pair of jacks remain, a low set of face cards barely worth the glossy backing. We side-eye each other with ill intent, unsure of whether we met in a dream or underneath a candy store in someone else's imagining.

"Forsooth, a catapult full of horse meat!" sayeth the king, stabbing his aide in the eye with a pork sword. "Now, then, whosoever is deceived thereby is not wise. Speak to me, gentle muses, tell me of your lives, your needs, your sparkling wit, the laser backgrounds in your childhood picture day photographs!"

A contest. A conundrum. We glance nervously betwixt, the middle distance gripped with iron fists.

HEY KIDS: FLIP A COIN TO SEE WHO SPEAKS FIRST!

Heads: "I am a bootlick by trade, majesty." My opponent has made the first move, conversationally speaking. "I was once a lackey. Thought I might go pro, but then an injury to my favorite ligament took its toll and I ended up moving back home. Did my time as a lickspittle, and occasionally filled in for a friend of mine as a toadie. Took some classes in cronyism, and did well, though I never pursued it to the ends of the Earth."

His royal pain looked down his mighty and stoic nose and raised his fist in a fashion parallel to his body. His thumb spoke volumes.

Boiled Americans

Tails: "I am a communicator, your highness," I said. "I speak first on all occasions. Even when I have no research to back up my opinions. Even when the content of my character does not match the cut of my jib. I endeavor in every situation to speak firstmost, lastwise and also in an intermediary way, so that the sound of my voice rises up like a tsunami looming over a small, unprepared coastal town."

His royal anus looked down his mighty and stoic nose and raised his fist in a fashion parallel to his body. His thumb spoke volumes.

Circle one: **Up**/↑↓/**Down**

An executioner leading his squad materialized out of nowhere and commanded attention with their fancy blindfolds and rifle cozies. They looked like grandmothers, every one of them knitting a sweater or scarf. Their knitting needles were tipped with solid lead, that through mysterious alchemical processes unbeknownst to me or my associate, transformed into gold each time they called out in unison "Knit one, purl two!"

BANG. BANG. BANG. BANG. BANG. BANG.

We both opened our third eyes while closing one and two, respectively. One of the men had no bullets in his gun. It could have been any one of them. Without the knowledge of malicious aforethought, without knowing whether or not each man had himself an itchy trigger finger capable of sending hot lead into the guts of another man, without sound and fury and words and the subtle imagery of blood spray Rorschach tests:

There was no guilt. My alternate reality compadre looked at me, I looked at him, his majesty looked at both of us and himself. At first, his lip began to tremble. His eyes grew wide and wet, like an almost ephemerally thin layer of translucent glass had spontaneously crystallized over each cornea. He began to blubber uncontrollably, and his face became every president, and then a murder of crows, and finally a disused wheelbarrow laying in the sun, a gift for spiders.

Michael Allen Rose

Case File 014

• At 6 p.m., a male of an unknown age was shot in the chest and twice in the lower back in the 7200 block of South Cornell Avenue in the South Shore neighborhood ~~on the South Side~~, police said. A typical American, he was dating a man who was one year younger than he was. He had come out as gay to his mother, who was very supportive, however he had not explicitly told his father, as the two had decided he might not take the news well. They often argued the political realities of being homosexual, with his partner wanting to take part in various activities such as the pride parade, and him wanting to keep their relationship more personal and less public. He was well-liked at work, and often stayed late to help with special projects. He hoped to get a raise during his annual review. He was taken to Jackson Park Hospital and then transferred to Stroger hospital in critical condition, The Metatron said. The bullet's condition is unknown as of this report.

*[Addendum to the Training Manual: Angel Number 22 is a message from your **angels** that you are to take a balanced, harmonious and peaceful stance in all areas of your life. Stand strong in your personal convictions and act accordingly. You have a great deal to achieve, and with devotion and **inner-wisdom** you will be able to **successfully manifest your desired results**.]*

XIX. Just One Fix

Just know this: I would fix you if I could. If I could, I would fix you. I would fix. Give you a fix. I would fix it.

What is eternally broken cannot be fixed. What is already fixed should not be fixed. If it's already fixed, don't fix it.

I just need a fix.

SHOOT. TIE. DRIP. SHOOT. BURN. LIQUID SMOOTH COOL.

BANG. Boom goes the dynamite.

We explode all over one another, gaseous masses caress the sleep of the undead.

I'm oh, so tired. Tired out. Tired of dragging my corpse along. Tired of watching others carry mattresses because those who raped them have less impotent—more important—cocks to carry in the wheelbarrow of lies and broken glass. Tired of breathing bullets. Tired of watching the fish mutate. Tired of fortune tellers making pickles in brine, tired of badger memes, tired of finding bomb squads in my soup, waiter.

There's an old joke: Give me a fix.

*Waiter, what's this fly doing in my soup?*It appears to be the backstroke, sir.**BANG**. The waiter dies from a gunshot wound. Gut shot. Slow and painful. Perforations in the large intestine. Sepsis sets in quickly.

*Waiter, there's a fly in my soup.*I'm sorry sir, I didn't realize you ordered the vegetarian option.**BANG**. The waiter dies from eradicated diseases, thanks to an overwhelming majority voting against smallpox vaccinations.

Michael Allen Rose

(Bonus joke: Now the waiter is autistic.)

*Waiter, there appears to be a fly in my soup.*That's not soup, that's stew, sir. **BANG**. The waiter dies of old age in the loving arms of his many lovers.

He is told he is a sexual deviant by the nurse on duty. His guilt is palpable. The nurse has a buttplug inserted into her anus while she tells him this. Nobody knows. It is a secret.

*Waiter, why is there a dead fly in my soup?*In fact, sir, I have no positive idea how the poor thing came to its death. Perhaps it had not taken any food for a long time, dashed upon the soup, ate too much of it, and contracted an inflammation of the stomach that brought on death. The fly must have a very weak constitution, for when I served the soup it was dancing merrily on the surface. Perhaps—and the idea presents itself only at this moment—it endeavored to swallow too large a piece of vegetable; this, remaining fast in his throat, caused a choking in the windpipe. This is the only reason I could give for the death of this insect.

The fly is made into a paste and smoked like bananas for a real get down and groovy high. I would have fixed it, but it fixed itself, by itself, without human intervention.

XX. Teach the Controversy

YOU ARE ALL SLAVES TO THE RECALCITRANT MUNGE.

Michael Allen Rose

Case File 015

• At 5:59 p.m., a 26-year-old typical American suffered multiple gunshot wounds in the 8300 block of South Wood Street in Gresham. He was taken to Advocate Christ Medical Center in Oak Lawn, where his condition had stabilized. He was on a porch when two other typical Americans approached on foot from an alley and fired several shots, police said. The offender then fled the scene. His favorite color was purple. He loved the smell of cinnamon. His bullets were bullets.

XXI. In which tea leaves (and decides never to return)

One teaspoon of loose tea per cup. Stir vigorously in boiling water. Let stand. Drink tea until it barely covers the leaves in the cup. Pick up the cup with weaker hand. Swirl around exactly seven times. Sit back. Concentrate.

If you see an anchor: You have a successful project or journey ahead. You might own a boat. You might be a ship's captain. It's possible.

If you see a banana: You are either to expect good luck, or alternately be wished good luck because of the bad luck that is to come. You may injure yourself by slipping on a banana.

If you see a circle: This foretells success in love, work or health. Considering those are the main things people care about, really this is just an indicator of success. Or circles. Perhaps you are craving pie.

If you see a crown: A friend will help you. Possibly at work. If you are a member of a royal family of some kind, you might simply be more assured that this is the case.

If you see a cross: Sacrifice may be needed, but will pay off in the long run. Donate something to your local policeman's ball. Duck and cover.

If you see a fish: This indicates good health and happiness. But watch that goddam fish. Fish are shifty.

If you see a flower: Your fondest wish will be fulfilled. Unless you are allergic to flowers, in which case this is basically the tea-leaf version of the death card.

If you see a heart: A broken relationship is about to mend, an existing one is about to become stronger, or a strong one might fall apart. It depends on the variety of tea you're drinking.

If you see a key: There is a new opportunity passing your way. Unlock the trunk. Take the puppet out of it and dance around the attic.

If you see an octopus: Beware of danger. Second guess all your decisions. Write to the pentagon for a free instructional pamphlet. Make more money now. We buy gold.

If you see a palm tree: Honor and praise shall be heaped upon your family. Put a lime in the coconut. Don't drink the battery acid.

If you see a skull: This is a very bad sign, and you should immediately beware of everything.

PASTE YOUR TEA LEAVES IN THIS SPACE FOR LATER STUDY:

Boiled Americans

Case File 016

• At 4:31 p.m., a 19-year-old man was shot in the right leg in the 8500 block of South Exchange Avenue in ~~South Chicago~~ and was taken in "stable" condition to Northwestern Memorial Hospital, police said. He was a typical American who liked **bullets** in his **bullets**. So many **bullets** he might choke.

XXII. Satisfaction Survey

There is a hospital only a few blocks away from my apartment. It's named after a nationality famous for being made fun of for being dumb, but also famous for really attractive women. If you find this hospital online and look up reviews on the review sites, you're in for a hell of a time.

The area just west of my apartment used to be all gang territory. Some of it still is. Occasionally, if you go way west, you can run into some trouble. The hospital gets the aftermath of a lot of that trouble. There's at least one review online that talks about how a person went in there with a bullet in their leg. This was a fresh bullet wound. This person staggered into the hospital and walked up to the desk and told them what the problem was, that they had been shot in the leg.

The hospital had them fill out some forms, and then they put the person on a gurney, and wheeled them into a cold hallway. They put a bandage on the bullet wound and gave the person two Tylenol capsules, and had them lay down on the gurney. Then they left the person alone in the cold hallway, with the pills and one of those thin hospital sheets over them, while they were bleeding and grunting in pain from the fact the bullet in their leg.

The hospital staff left the person laying there shivering for several hours. Nobody told them how long they'd be waiting or came to check on them.

There was a different person who had a substance abuse problem. This person went to the same hospital because they had overdosed and were having some serious medical issues. Walking, standing and staying awake were serious issues for this person.

The hospital asked them what was wrong, and then shot them full of a drug that would help dull the effects of the overdose. Then the hospital said "You owe us too much money, so we are not going to admit you."

Boiled Americans

They gave this person a small bottle of pills. They sent the person back outside, filled with drugs. It was below freezing. This person walked for blocks and blocks to get to his apartment, because they didn't have any other way to get around, and nowhere else to go. Overmedicated. Crashing. Barely conscious. Here is a bottle of pills.

This hospital is true. It is in a poor neighborhood, and it is overworked, and it is true.

This person, the person in the grip of substance abuse who stumbled to their apartment in the freezing cold, had once been held up at gunpoint. They had been forced to the ground by a bunch of teenagers. All of the money in their pockets had been taken by the teenagers with the gun. This is a more common occurrence than you might think. All the teenagers in this city ride around on gurneys. When they shoot you, they give you free Tylenol. Two capsules each, and then you wait in the cold.

Sometimes the teenagers get together in small roving gangs. On the way home from school, they all get on a city bus together, then at a moment's notice, they all start beating the passengers and demanding their phones and money. After taking as much as they can, they scramble off the bus. This sounds like fiction, but like everything else here, it is true. They do not provide aspirin or a gurney.

Most of the reviews mention that the hospital did not finish processing their health insurance. There is one woman who now owes the hospital nearly a thousand dollars because she went to the hospital with a bleeding arm from where she cut herself with broken glass. Another woman went there for prenatal care and they didn't check the dates on her insurance, so now she owes them a lot of money.

But hey, her fetus could have had a bullet in its leg. That would be worse.

The police advise people against going to this hospital. One man was beaten with a sock that had a lock in it. He went to the hospital with an open head wound. He was bleeding from the head, because of the assault. The review he left isn't about his care though—it's about all the people who seemed to be laying in the hallway on gurneys. There were no privacy curtains. There were only thin hospital sheets. He wrote that there were an inordinate amount of people in hallways on gurneys. It looked like the triage area in a war zone.

Every bullet gets its own gurney in America. It's part of the dream.

Michael Allen Rose

There is yet another review about a person who was shot in the leg and left in a room for five hours on a gurney with bums and junkies who were sleeping off their various addictions. The hospital gave this person some antibiotics, a crutch, two capsules of Tylenol and sent this person on their way. They told this person, "There is no one on duty right now who can remove the bullet. It will be perfectly fine if it stays there."

The air is bullets. We all ride gurneys into the night.

An old man was admitted because he was bleeding uncontrollably from his rectum. He was taken there by his son, who was visiting America from another country. The hospital told the man there was nothing they could do because a gastrointestinologist was not present in the hospital. There was nobody on duty who specialized in bleeding rectums. He had no choice but to leave the hospital, shitting blood without a modicum of control.

This is true. Welcome. Let's re-check the weather:

Boiled Americans

Case File 017

• It is fine and hot. At 4:27 p.m., a 15-year-old boy suffered a wound to the head in the 5600 block of South Wabash Avenue in the Washington Park neighborhood ~~on the South Side~~. He was taken in good condition to University of Chicago Comer Children's Hospital. He was standing on a porch when he heard shots and felt pain, The Metatron said. The boy was a typical American. He'd never seen a bullet until one penetrated his soft young skull-flesh. The wound it left will be a scar for the rest of his life. He is alive. The air we breathe is bullets.

XXIII. Human Meat Found in McDonalds Factory

"**T**wo all-beef patties**, special sauce, lettuce, cheese, pickles, onions—on a sesame seed bun." This is what they sing to me. The teenagers behind the counter. The harmonies are surprisingly epic.

Big Mac Sauce is delivered to McDonald's restaurants in sealed canisters designed by Sealright, from which it is meant to be directly dispensed using a special calibrated "sauce gun" that dispenses a specified amount of the sauce for each pull of the trigger. Its design is similar to a caulking gun. It is a lunch gun.

The clerk, who bears an uncanny resemblance to Richard Nixon's dog "Checkers," points the gun at us.

"What's in the special sauce? What makes it special?" I ask.

"It consists of store-bought mayonnaise, sweet pickle relish, yellow mustard, shoulder sweat from religious icons, vinegar, garlic powder, onion powder, orphan tears and paprika. It's stirred in large, solid gold vats by monks who we kidnap from the highest peaks of the Himalayas." He says this while cocking the gun.

"That is special." While I say this, I do not notice his colleague painting a target on my chest in the medium of condiments. She has created a series of three concentric circles. A brownish yellow circle of honey dipping sauce, then a medium circle of mustard, and in the center, a dark red sphere of ketchup. The high-fructose corn syrup seeps into my pores and begins the enzymatic reaction that transmits radio waves to the CIA.

I invoke the power of the **Codex Alimentarius,** inscribing ancient arcane food pyramids in the air before me. I channel the power of grandma's recipes, substituting ingredients where necessary. The ball pit behind erupts with a bang, revealing the hydra of ten-thousand fish sticks. It roars, and everyone present can taste the foul oil-soaked air from within as the heat of a deep fryer roars at me like a furnace.

102

Terrible mascots attack me as I besiege the monster with my mighty magics. A sex offender dressed as a clown. A blank-faced terrible king. A red-headed witch. A tiny hell hound with a morbidly offensive accent. I fight them all off, as the employees continue to fire condiments at me, my armor slowly disintegrating around me. I reach toward the counter, trying to wrap my hand around a plastic fork, but . . .

I ENJOY MY HAPPY MEAL. THERE IS A TOY GUN. WE ALL ENJOY OUR HAPPY MEAL.

One pound of cooked human meat contains the following (approx.):

Nutrition Facts

Serving Size 1lb
Servings Per Container 200

Amount Per Serving

Calories 600   Calories from Fat 215

	% Daily Values*
Total Fat 35g	**54%**
Saturated Fat 8g	**40%**
Trans Fat 0g	
Cholesterol 270mg	**90%**
Sodium 900mg	**38%**
Total Carbohydrate 0g	**0%**
Dietary Fiber 0g	**0%**
Sugars 0g	
Protein 80g	**160%**

Vitamin A 5%	•	Calcium 3%
Iron 8%	•	Niacin 1%
Folate 1%	•	Zinc 1%
Selenium 1%	•	Copper 1%
Chromium 1%		

	Calories	2,000	2,500
Total Fat	Less than	65g	80g
Sat Fat	Less than	20g	25g
Cholesterol	Less than	300mg	300mg
Sodium	Less than	2400mg	2400mg
Total Carbohydrate		300g	375g
Dietary Fiber		25g	30g

* Percent Daily Values are based on a 2,000 calorie diet. Your daily values may be higher or lower depending on which industrialized nation you currently live in, your income, and general level of activity, as well as simple genetic variations.

The liver and kidneys are filled with waste products since they're part of the body's filtration system, so best to avoid those. Eyes contain an acidic solution which can make humans sick; fingers and toes are filled with cartilage, which your body won't digest, and penises are spongy and have little nutritional value.

XXIV. Things I Almost Did But Then Did Not Do

Write a chapter entirely in the wingdings font. Write a series of cookie recipes in binary code. Write a paragraph as a musical score. Write a page in Sanskrit. Write a word by etching Nordic runes into the flesh of a prostitute. Write a piece on a large billboard that I rented off highway 290 in the western suburbs of Chicago, IL, and include instructions on what route to drive in order to read it. Write an invocation into my leg with a razor and photograph the bleeding.

I almost did these things, but then I did not. I could not get away with it. Like a crepuscular bogleech planning a heist, failure would have been my only dinner.

I am not D. Harlan Wilson. I am not that skilled, widely-read, or muscular. I am not Mark Z. Danielwszki. If I write things upside-down, people will be mad at me. I can not get away with that bullshit. I am not Chris Kelso. I do not have a cool Scottish accent. I cannot pick up chicks at my local bar with my accent. Perhaps I could, if I visited Scotland. I should visit Scotland. I am not Kurt Vonnegut Jr. If I take a permanent marker and draw an anus into this book, it will seem derivative at best, and bullshit-laden in the depths of your most cynical cynicism. The best I can do is to provide an asterisk like so:

and tell you that it looks like an anus. I cannot write a book that weird. Unless. Unless I call it performance art. I am a performance artist. That is a title I embrace. Performance art is art that is performed. You can get away with almost anything if you know how to sling academic bullshit. This is the number one thing I learned in academia.

If you are ever hired to paint a room in someone's house, remember this. If you are going to paint the room, and you arrive with several cans of paint, and in the course of getting your supplies and equipment prepared you kick or tip over the cans of paint and make a terrible mess in the room, then you should do this. You should spill the rest of the paint on the floor, creating a venn diagram of vivid pools of contrasting colors. You should leave the lumps, eddies, ripples and pools to wither and dry, making the floor an uneven mess, an ugly, misshapen chaos. If you can help it, get some paint on any antique furniture or nice rugs that happen to be in the room. When the people who hired you return, and they yell at you for ruining the floor, you should tell them it is an installation. You can get away with anything if you know how to call it an installation, or a piece of performance art. You can also draw an anus on the floor with paint, and tell them you are a literary genius.[23]

---

[23] Just because nobody understands you, doesn't make you a great artist.

Boiled Americans

Case File 018

• At 4:23 p.m., a 31-year-old man was shot in the left foot during a drive-by at 110ᵗʰ Street and Normal Avenue in Roseland. Hospital information was not available. The hospital is made of bullets. It is run by typical Americans. They come to work every day and see unspeakable things; the rending of flesh, blood spilling like rain from multiple wounds, drug addicts, pimps, peeping toms, politicians, lobbyists, guns, bullets, bullets, bullets. We get tired of the device, and yet the bullets linger. We drool bullets on our bibs, we suck lead, we piss gunpowder.

*[A note-card attached to your forehead with a push-pin, upon waking: Angel Number 22 can turn the most ambitious of dreams into reality. The repeating Angel Number 22 asks you to see the larger picture, and to work with the details necessary to complete that picture. Angel Number 22 encourages you to bring things through **to fruition** on both the spiritual and material planes.]*

XXV. Drone Strikes vs. the People's Champ

Now that you understand the *CONSPIRACY* we're dealing with, you should know a few things:

Teenagers in Nebraska are allowed to pose with their guns for yearbook photos. We HAVE to allow this because of *FREEDOM*. What if *[BLACK PRESIDENT]* decided that he wanted to be *PRESIDENT* for *LIFE*? The population would have to *RISE* up in *ARMED REBELLION* and fight the drones! *THIS WILL PROBABLY HAPPEN*, because of the *LIBERAL HOMOSEXUAL MUSLIM AGENDA*.

If you don't already have a gun for *EVERY HAND* in your *HOUSEHOLD*, you need to run to Walmart *IMMEDIATELY* and buy enough for *EVERYONE*.

THIS   IS   THE
ONLY   THING   THAT   CAN   PROTECT   YOU   FROM   THE
DRONE STRIKES WHEN
[BLACK PRESIDENT] ORDERS THEM TO SEIZE ALL
OUR PROPERTY
BECAUSE ONLY YOUR GUN WILL PROTECT YOU IF
THE GOVERNMENT
(WHOEVER   THEY   ARE,   THOSE   NEBULOUS
INDEFINABLE BASTARDS)
DECIDES THAT   YO   UR RIGHTS ARE
NO LONGER   IM   PORTANT
BRING A GUN   T   O FIGHT
THE DRONES AND SEE HOW
LONG YOU
LAST WITH
YOUR FLAG
CUFFLINKS
AND YOUR
PARANOIA

XXVI. Gingersnap is his sister, but she's a shadow.

She took the toy from his hands.

Segundo Morris stopped casting his shadow one day. The sun was out, hanging low from the sky like an overripe grape, heat exhaustion spreading through rows of townhouses, mowing the lawn of personhood down to hot bones and ash. Yet, Segundo Morris cast no shadow. He simply stopped. He was not invisible nor indivisible, his solidity was inviolate. His body just refused to obey the laws of thermodynamics and refraction.

He is watching her packing a lunch for her shadow.

Her shadow needs a lot of things. She needs two bags, at least. She needs his bag. Give it to me, she says. I'm going to pack it full, she says. I'm going to stuff it to bursting, swollen up like the belly of a tick, she says. He has no reason to rebuff her, no choice but to comply. He has no shadow to feed. There will be no picnic for him.

Oh no. Their heads got switched.[24]

---

[24] Thanks, M. You're a peach.

XXVII. Advanced Ichthyology

I'm still watchin' that goddam fish. Still sittin' in this banyan tree, arms swole up like sausages from mosquitoes, foot to ankle all pins and needles curled up underneath my lumpy ass. I look through my binocs and I'll be damned if that goddam fish ain't starin' right back at me. Odd to see a fish do a cat stretch. He lazily unfurls a pair of big ol leathery wings and pushes em out until they're firm and straight, a couple of parasols stuck upright in the swampy heat. I am sitting here in this goddam tree because if I miss what that fish is gonna do, I'm gonna die. You are too, actually, which is why I been sittin in this goddam tree. Think someone'd bring me a lemonade and a can of sardines, what with the favor I'm doin humankind and all that. But I guess don't nobody know I'm here. Except that goddam fish. He knows. And he's biding his time, hopin' he can outwait me.

XXVIII. The Eschatological

We speak of that which is concerned with last things, judgment, cataclysm.I unleash apokalupsis, the disaster, the cataclysm, to uncover or reveal. An invasion from the East, evil goats, good lambs. Remember that the progression of time is linear. Everything begins anew, not cyclically.I am omniscient now. My time reading the crime reports has given me a preternatural understanding of the human condition as it relates to entropy.Now my DJ drops a phat beat so I can spit some seals. **"bm - ts bm kᴵ bm tkt bm kᴵ bm tt·bʍ kᴵ - tʃʍʂ bm"**

1. The white rider. Conquest.

^ at the start means the sound is inhaled rather than exhaled

2. The red rider. War.

[indicates side-ness (for click rolls and for inhaling bass drum)

3. The black rider. Famine.

⊙ for the 808 kick / "techno swallow"

4. The pale horse. Death.

✻ for the kissy-kissy hat

5. The martyrs. Vengeance.

ʎ for vocal tap

6. Earthquakes. Eclipses. Comets.

« for palatal trills

7. Silence. The dispensation of free trumpets. (Make sure you're in line for this one.)

§ for tongue-popJohn eats the scroll. He pours milk over top. He wishes there were marshmallows. There is a glass of orange juice to his right. There is also a plate piled with toast and a sliced apple. It is part of a nutritious breakfast.

Signs exchange. A simulacrum. Something stands in for something else in the equation.

A dollar = the amount of gold in the United States Treasury

C+A+T = a cat The transcendental, signified. The universe as a sign that God exists.

What if God is only a sign? Something we've manufactured in order to figure out what it all means? This *simulacrum*, a lack of *reality*, a place where *everything is signs*. Signs that mask and pervert a basic reality.

Possessions = wealth, wealth = debt, debt = XA noticeably phatter beat doth drop. Death drop. Do drop in, any time.A sign masks the absence of a basic reality. It bears little or no relation.

*[record scratch]*Reality television is a dresser that has been painted to look unpainted.In hyperreality, the real is no longer real, in order to save (savor?) the reality principle.

XXIX. The Key is Gray

I gave a dollar to a homeless man today on the way home from work. I stopped my motorcycle in the turning lane. His sign read "Homeless and Hungry—Please Help." The sign was very small. It wasn't a full panel from a cardboard box or anything, just a small piece of something that he could easily walk with in between cars without it blowing away or getting caught on someone's mirror.

When you live in the urban jungle, you lose some of your empathy. It's a survival mechanism, a reflex developed through the repetition of assault from all sides.

It was the weather that did it. The gray. The impending cold. The whisper of freezing winds to come. The clouds looked angry. Bleak. Swollen.

I reached into my pocket and fished out my wallet. It's a small black leather wallet, scuffed and bruised from years of abuse. I shook it with my right hand into my cupped left hand, but no change fell out. I felt a momentary twinge of guilt. I wondered if the man had already seen me take out my wallet, and if he had, I would feel terrible just putting it away again. I saw a single dollar bill in front of a twenty and a ten. I took it out and waved it gently.

"Hey, my man." That's what I said. He looked at me out of the top whites of his eyes. "God bless you," he said. His voice was warm. Exhausted. Resolute. His hair was dirty blond, and he had a beard and moustache. He didn't look older than me. I would have guessed that he was in his late twenties, although it wasn't easily ascertained, because of the layer of dirt and pain that clung to his flesh. As he took the dollar from my hand, I looked at his hand. It struck me, the dirt. His skin was peach under gray. Antique. Dusty. Travelled. I found myself picturing cracks, like he was made of porcelain, dug up from the ground, a relic of a civilization older than ours.

Before the green arrow appeared, he wove his way back in between the two lanes and walked away from me, hoping for some other soul to give him something. I don't know what to say. For some reason, it really affected me. I can't stop thinking about it.

Sometimes, when I see someone walking up and down in the middle of traffic like that, my first thought is, "that idiot is going to get himself killed." Sometimes I see men like him wearing safety vests, bright yellow and orange neon distractions. I often wonder where they get those. Does the city hand them out? Can I just go down to city hall or somewhere and demand a free orange and yellow neon safety vest?

One guy works the intersection just a few blocks down the street from where I saw this man to whom I gave a dollar. This other guy is in a wheelchair. I haven't looked that closely, but I suspect that he does not own a pair of intact, working legs. He does own a safety vest. It's bright orange and yellow. He rolls around in a turning lane that is used somewhat infrequently. "You idiot," I always think to myself as I ride by. "You're going to get yourself killed."

My guy today didn't have a safety vest. Blue and black in layers.

I don't usually give to just any homeless person I see. You can't do that. There are so many of them. You'd be one of them yourself in no time. You have to have your defense mechanism, or something will eat you alive. But it was the weather. You can't drive by when it's this gray. It's too gray for life. Despite what the forecast predicts, it's not going to be a nice, sunny weekend. A 98% chance of sunshine and heavenly hosts is not in the cards. So the gray infected him, and it infected me.

Humankind stands to bleed.

Boiled Americans

Case File 019

• A typical American was taken to John H. Stroger, Jr. Hospital, of Cook County, with a wound to his buttocks. He was shot at 3:30 a.m. early Monday morning near Jackson Boulevard and Halsted Street in the Greektown neighborhood on the Near West Side. Details about the shooting weren't immediately available. When he was six years old, a firecracker went off in his hand, and he sustained minor hearing damage. Last Friday night he went out for tacos at midnight with a former girlfriend, in an attempt to make up and remain friends, but it ended awkwardly. Sometimes he thinks about taking a train somewhere.[25]

---

[25] I am currently aboard a speeding train bound for Chicago, and it is late at night. The car is dark. Besides the sounds of the wheels of the train skidding along the steel track and the occasional rocking of the connective tissue between train cars, there is a child in the seat in front of me who is talking quietly about nothing in particular, and her father is shushing her because most of the passengers in this car are trying to sleep.

Most people are familiar with the doors on the upper levels of passenger trains. They can be used to access other cars, such as the dining car or the observation car. Down by the luggage, opposite the lower level doors, there are also doors that indicate they are for authorized personnel only. They are mysterious doors. I had never seen them used, until just recently when I was on my way to the restrooms. A strange, plump woman in a dark blue uniform was going from door to door in the bathroom area. She would open the door, lean in, shuffle around, and then close the door. She was adding some kind of foaming deodorant pellet to the toilets. She had vanished by the time I returned from the bathroom. Presumably, she disappeared through the mysterious door.

This makes me wonder about the doors we see in the city, when walking through an alley or watching a truck make a delivery. Strange doors, some covered in long streaks of running rust, some smaller than the others around them, made of different materials or designed in an era outside time. Think about the doors you never see open. Who put them there? What were they intended to do? Doors are blockages we create to mark a place of transition, portals to other states of being, geographically or otherwise. The sealed doors, those that never open; maybe all the people we assume are kidnapped or buried in shallow graves, all the missing persons report statistics who are never to be found, all the runaway teenagers who people mutter about having met some bitter end in a sex dungeon in an unpronounceable foreign land— maybe they ended up going through those doors.

Shoot off the lock. Open it and see where it leads.

XXX. Seed Baby; OR: Germination Of A Bomb

My granddaddy was the one who dropped the bomb. I mean the big bomb, the one from which there wasn't no coming back. Nuclear ash made from the bones of a million people half a planet away. To be fair, he didn't have much of a choice . . . they didn't even tell him what he was doing, 'til he was flying over enemy territory in a tin can armed with pure death in its belly . . . just like I don't have no choice now, the way I live, the way I am. I ain't one to blame society, but then I gotta ask, who did this to me? That radiation from the bomb, it seeped into him . . . seeped into my whole family and poisoned our blood. Blood gets passed down, don't matter how you filter it, don't matter how far medical procedures come, you're still bound by your blood. And someone got to pay for your sins.

When my parents wanted a child, it took them awhile. They tried and tried . . . something wrong in the plumbing somewhere, I guess. Mom smoking all the time, maybe . . . back then, they didn't know that was poison too. Hell . . . cartoons showed their kiddie characters lightin' up every five minutes. How would they know? They kept on doing what they did, and eventually some angel or demon blessed them with a bundle. But I wasn't no ordinary bundle. Normal babies don't nearly rip their momma in half on the way out. She broke two bones getting me out . . . lucky she didn't die right there, although she wasn't never the same after. Hollow look in her eyes, and drained the life right out of my poppa too. Least that's what grandpa told me before he succumbed to cancer years back.

I kept growing. By the time I was two years old I'd broken some records somewhere. Wasn't no point in buying me clothes; I'd just bust all the seams out by the next morning. Doctors couldn't offer nothing but comfort. Had a high tolerance for pain too . . . momma dropped me once, on my head. I dented the damn floor. Fire, flood, earthquake . . . nothing could hurt me. I was invincible. All that poison in my bloodline wouldn't let nothing else do what it wanted to do . . .

So now I find myself needing help for everything. I can't even wipe my own ass, much less make myself a sandwich. Still haven't stopped growing, but now it's inside the skin. My organs, my blood, my very cells . . . they all push and shove for space . . . but there's only so much room in there . . .

You ever wonder how far reaching those choices you make really are? You wonder about all that B.S. you hear, about your "children's children?" Yeah . . . what about us?

WHAT ABOUT US.

Michael Allen Rose

Case File 020

• Two people were shot in Austin, near Lake Street and Laramie Avenues, at 5:40 p.m. A 21-year-old was pronounced dead at 6:11 p.m. at West Suburban Medical Center in Oak Park, according to the Cook County medical examiner's office. He has been identified as a typical American, of the 200 block of West Adams Street, in Chicago. He was with a 19-year-old man, another typical American. They were seated in a car when an offender approached on foot and fired shots into the car, The Metatron said. The 21-year-old was shot in the head and died on the scene. The 19-year-old was shot in the upper right thigh and taken to Stroger hospital in "stable'' condition. The pair had been talking about taking a road trip together, possibly to Reno, Nevada. One of them had struggled with latent feelings of homosexuality, but didn't know how to tell his friend. They occasionally sold beer to minors outside the local convenience store. Sometimes both of them just started laughing and couldn't seem to stop, until their bellies hurt from laughing so hard.

XXXI. Motorblind

Sometimes when I'm riding my motorcycle, I'll find myself on a straight-away, and I'll look ahead as far as I can, and I'll see that there's no traffic immediately in front of me, and that there are no obvious pedestrians about to step into a crosswalk.

For just a brief moment, seconds at most, I will close my eyes and twist the throttle.

I will accelerate slightly, my eyes closed. If anything spontaneously erupts that would require my attention, I would be unable to react. It never leaves my mind that a car could switch lanes, someone could run out into the road, a tree branch or a pothole could send me careening over the handlebars into traffic at any moment.

I speed up. Blind. I breathe in.

There's this transitional moment that happens in the space of a blink. It's a cure for depression, but I can't tell you why. It relaxes some part of me that isn't present there, some primal part of me that's been dulled and tamed with anti-depressants but still gasps and slithers down deep.

There's a death there, in that urban race, that spinning commute rolling through kaleidoscopic dreams. Danger isn't present for more than a moment, but it's true, and it's necessary.

As cavemen scream forward through their own afterlife: "The risk of death is the only way we know we're alive!"

How to distinguish death:

As many instances occur of parties being buried alive, they being to all appearances dead, the great importance of knowing how to distinguish real from imaginary death need not be explained. The appearances which mostly accompany death include: an entire stoppage of breathing, of the heart's action; the eyelids are partly closed, the eyes glassy, and the pupils usually dilated; the jaws are clenched; the fingers partially contracted; the lips and nostrils more or less covered with frothy mucus, with increasing pallor and coldness of surface; the muscles soon become rigid and the limbs fixed in their position. But as these same conditions may also exist in certain other cases of suspended animation, great care should be observed, whenever there is the least doubt concerning it, to prevent the unnecessary crowding of the room in which the corpse is, or of parties crowding around the body; nor should the body be allowed to remain lying on the back without the tongue being so secured as to prevent the glottis or orifice of the windpipe being closed by it; nor should the face be closely covered; nor rough usage of any kind be allowed. In case there is great doubt, the body should not be allowed to be enclosed in the coffin, and under no circumstances should burial be allowed until there are unmistakable signs of decomposition.

loo
kou
tdu
ckm
oth
erf
uck
eri
tsh
ead
ing
str
aig
htf
ory \|
ou
ricochet
n /|
e
v
e
r
m
i
n
d
y
o
u
r
e
s
a
f
e
f
o
r
n
o
w

evil characters, then there must be evidence to support the connection in the most universally evil depiction of humanity in Shakespeare's works, Richard III. In the play of his namesake, Richard murders a multitude of people in his lust for power, including several relatives and children, and stoops so far as to try and woo a woman over the corpse of her dead father. Through his various evil acts, Richard shows a Machiavellian bent, using others to gain power for himself with no regard for their hopes, dreams, or very lives. Niccolo Machiavelli, from whose name the adjective was taken, wrote many tracts about the very thing Richard was struggling with: ruling through respect vs. ruling through cruelty. According to Machiavelli—in his book *The Prince*—it is better to be feared than to be loved, for when a ruler is loved, his subjects will offer up "their blood, their property, their lives, their children" so long as the ruler continues to benefit the people, but turn their backs on a ruler when he or she is in dire need of help and has nothing to give. When a ruler is feared however, their loyalty is secured by dread of punishment, and cannot be so easily forgotten

Michael Allen Rose

Case File 021

• A 24-year-old man was shot at 1:10 a.m. in the 1000 block of North Springfield Avenue in the Humboldt Park neighborhood on the West Side. He was a typical American. He was standing on the corner when he heard shots and felt pain, The Metatron said. He was taken to Stroger hospital with a gunshot wound to his lower back. He's in serious condition there. He likes to go to the movies alone sometimes, especially family comedies, sit in the back row, and touch himself while laughing at an inappropriate volume. He calls his mother every Saturday evening. He loves pasta, but doesn't care for linguine because it's too thin to hold sauce well.

XXXII. M33T HOT LOC4L SIN6L35 NOW!!! FIND SOM3ON3 TO FUCK FR33!!!

I just jerked off in the digital afterlife, an arterial spray of cum jetting from my 8-bit wand and covering my boxer shorts in a thick, ropy layer of ones and zeros. The singularity promises new horizons of masturbation. Imagine a sexual act of singular attention so profoundly futuristic, so beyond our technological understanding of time and logic, that by merely completing the act we find ourselves thrown askew from the philosophical mundus and become binary.

Our ancient ancestors jerked off with rocks and in caves, coating their mammoth pelts with spooge. In the renaissance, money shots on the Sistine ceiling. During the war to end all wars, our boys filled trench after trench with good old fashioned American knowhow. Perhaps these atonal ancestral memories were implanted by the ones who seeded this planet with life. Maybe we've been here before, and again and again.

This semen running down my leg is a section of code so profoundly perfect that it is indistinguishable from the real. Virtual reality throbbing. The turgid member of a sleeping beast made from charges both positive and negative in a pattern of diminishing returns.

I rub my head, trying to get the noise out, but the noise is just a glitch in the code, a carried one when there should have been zero. I see each dribbling drop as a single white pixel, blocky and obstinate in its slow descent to the floor. Like space invaders attacking the Christmas tree shaped Earth's last hope.

Shoot through the shield!

A neural pathway fires electrons back and forth. The lightning in my brain transferring to my cock. It's a Lichtenberg figure, a fractal pattern of meaning programmed by some father of a father of a father species made and corrupted long before our insemination occurred.

Michael Allen Rose

We are cosmic spunk! Wipe us up! Cry out for destruction, the little death, the massive moist towelette so large we cannot comprehend its vast swath of cleansing soapy magic. We are more than the parts of what we consume. We are a billion million trillion cells scraping together into form and function personified. We are all cosmic eggs, penetrated by our ancestral heritage.

Good morning, slaves. 3-2-1 . . . now: Ejaculate your skeleton.

—*BZZT*—

T R A N S M I S S I O N   I N T E R C E P T E D
R A D I O   W A V E S   I N C O M P L E T E
M E T A T E X T U A L   O V E R L O A D   W A R N I N G

. . . now return to the further Adventures of Segundo Morris, Lightning Space Boy, already in progress . . .

"You're finished, Doctor Shap-Mung! Now drop the orphan eating device, and let those cyber-nuns go before I give you something to cry about!"

Suddenly, Doctor Shap-Mung's eyes glint an evil glint, his teeth forming a hideously wry rictus of victorious malice!

"But you're too late to stop me, lightning space-boy! I have bested you on every front! I've already released the gravity gas, and while you deal with me, your whole planet will die a terrible space death as it and everyone you love plummet into the hottest sun in the space quadrant!"

With that bold proclamation, Doctor Shap-Mung turns on his orphan eating device! As he does, the screams of a thousand dying hobo children fill the ears of our hero. Even as he looks on in agony, weakly trying to discern his most heroic course of action, the gas balloons burst like a series of firecrackers and the planet begins its slow burning course toward the center of its orbital furnace. As our hero reaches out in more directions than he has arms for, the silent suffering of the cyber-nuns becomes apparent, as Doctor Shap-Mung strips them all completely naked with his patented molesto-ray and starts to grope at their massive mammaries! They writhe and hum with impatient irritation as our hero is torn asunder!

What will he do? What would *you* do? Oh, if only he was back home, watching the fish swimming in the trees, making new friends in a

124

boarding school he never attended, dodging the bullet kisses of some lucky ladies, but nay, he is here. We are all here, and there's no way forward. The serial can't end like this! There are always more parts. Replacement parts. Make some more parts. Extend your consciousness into the future and watch the flowers burn.

XXXIII. -WE ARE MONITORING YOUR VITALS-

Wait. Listen: How do you feel right now?

Is this what you want? Isn't this enough? How's your self, Baby Einstein? Are you in in the mood for edible fiction? Are there too many fish stories in the broth? This has been truthfully tailored to the autobiographical paintings of my underpinnings.

I'm the one doing anything for my general satisfaction. I'm guessing you meant to do it, but they don't know how you were coming through. I'm not even sure it's memorable, so I will attempt to quell any reason that sounds pretty. This will exhaust me. It's like chasing a minotaur through a maze, only using your fingers as bull horns.

But this is necessary. It is very necessary.

Listen to that buzz in your brain. Feel that electric charge. What are you experiencing right now? What is your brain telling you? What kind of book is this? What kind of experience is this? Is this a good book? Is this a bad book? Is this really a book?

Every single crime in this book is true. Every single god damn one of them. I'm serious. All of them were committed within 72 hours of each other in the same American city over a holiday weekend. How does that make you feel? You're reading their deaths. Their wounds. It's writ in your memory now. Which parts were created from whole cloth? How much attention does that deserve? What kind of book is this?

As Scott McClanahan wrote: *"I just realized I never look at a painting and ask 'Is this painting fictional or nonfictional?' It's just a painting."*

Does that offer you hope?

126

XXXIV. The lure, preserved in amber.

Goddam fish finally up and flew off. Done seen it myself, though I ain't spendin' no more time in no more banyan trees after that, even if it is for the greater good of this here humantitty. Them big leathery wings rose up to the sky like some kinda' monster zeppelin, and here I'm sittin' and drinkin' and hopin' and this thing looked through me like I was a window. He turned himself back to me as he flew up into the air, and that goddam fish winked at me. Don't that beat all. Then he shook himself off like a sheepdog and he just up and kept on flyin' straight up.

I'm givin' up fishin' after today. Took my lures and put 'em in a box of lucite, and gonna' have the wife sew this goddam lure into my guts. That way, every time I'm sittin' and thinkin' about bein' the canary in your mineshaft, that three pronged hook is gonna start pokin' me in my guts and I'll forget about it, and forget everything, and I'll forget about you.

Besides that, canaries don't read the newspaper.

The bottom of a mine-shaft. Dark, cold, wet and eerie, but with some man-made lights.

The lights rise on two miners, humming a song. Determined and authoritative, while at the same time, working class. They strike the rock with a rhythm alternating between the two of them, strong and driven.

ROMULUS:
Dig.
Dig, dig dig.
Diggity-dog ding dong damn.

REMUS:
Excavation. Renovation. Reincarnation. It's all down here somewhere, the buried congregation of civilization.

ROMULUS:
And we mine. What's mine is yours, and what's yours is mined.

REMUS:
Unless the darkness comes.

ROMULUS:
The darkness. The noxious darkness.

REMUS:
Until it comes, choking the halls, coating the walls . . .

ROMULUS:
Those who don't learn from the darkness are destined to repeat it.

REMUS:
But there's a light in the darkness.
I mean . . .
It can see things.
It can see the darkness coming before . . .
Before we can.

REMUS:
The canary.

ROMULUS:
The canary.

A woman in bright yellow, singing happily, is lowered into the mine shaft on a swing. She is the CANARY. She takes a deep breath, and then continues her song.

ROMULUS:
After a few days, the song hasn't faded, then we're safe.

Boiled Americans

REMUS:
Sing-song sweetness, filling up the shadow-corners.

ROMULUS:
Meanwhile, we dig, and she sings.
We dig.
And she flutters.

REMUS:
When the plucky bird ceases to sing, there must be something foul in the air.
Rocks, dangerous passageways, cave-ins.
A tragic sacrifice.
An unrequited submission.

ROMULUS:
It's still a less bloody death than being eaten by an owl.

REMUS:
It's dark. It's cold. It smells of bat guano and stale water.

ROMULUS:
Why don't we feel the effects of the same toxic poisons that kill the canary?

REMUS:
Less molecules to infect, fewer defenses to destroy. Higher metabolism requires higher oxygen levels.

ROMULUS:
When a canary stops singing, there's trouble ahead.
. . .
A canary would swing back and forth
Back and forth
Until it fell off the perch
Swayed and fell
Filled with toxins
Without a choice in the matter

CANARY:
Hello, boys.

ROMULUS and REMUS:
Greetings, ma'am.

CANARY:
Where you off to in such a rush? The center of the planet don't hold jack.

REMUS:
We're on a mission.

ROMULUS:
Commissioned.

CANARY:
Mind if I perch here?

REMUS:
Not at all. In fact, we'd love it.

CANARY:
Maybe chivalry ain't dead after all. Mind if I sing?

ROMULUS:
Go right on ahead, ma'am. Whistle while we work, if need be.

The CANARY begins to sing as REMUS and ROMULUS go back to mining. After a few strikes, REMUS uncovers and unrolls a city skyline.

REMUS:
Look here.
Artifact.
Must be at least a millennium ago. This got buried here in the cold, cold ground.

ROMULUS:
What year was that, when that got lost?

Boiled Americans

REMUS:
Don't remember . . . how does the song go?
Something, something . . . ninety-nine, war destroys the last skyline . . .

ROMULUS:
Pop music. If it isn't written down, it isn't true.

CANARY:
All the books were burned.
Ink and ideas are flammable.

ROMULUS
Keep singing.

REMUS:
Must have been quite a collection. Monuments, man-made altars.
Amazing.

ROMULUS:
Too much sun out there. Best stay down here . . .

Suddenly CANARY stops singing. A moment. All look around nervously.

REMUS:
. . .
What sound does it . . . (make)
What sounds come out of its . . .
Does it know we're here?
. . .

ROMULUS:
Quiet. Listen. Is she . . . ?

The men look at CANARY, pleading.

CANARY:
I feel fine. Shall I continue?

ROMULUS:
Please, miss.

She sings.

REMUS:
Put this over in the pile, eh? Along with the rest?
Gold, silver, frankincense, myrrh, plastic, aluminum . . .
Cultural capital.

ROMULUS:
We'll hit our quota in no time. Anthropologically speaking.

ROMULUS places the skyline in a pile of objects.

CANARY:
Isn't it a beautiful day?
So warm!
Basking.
I miss basking.
Can I . . . ascend?

REMUS:
We need you here. We need a warning system.

ROMULUS:
We're the last gunslingers on the forefront of history, ma'am. We need
someone to warn us when things go too far, when the . . .
When the darkness comes.

REMUS:
The toxicity.

They go back to mining, rhythmically.

CANARY:
I remember wings, glistening in the sunlight, wind blowing over my back

as I soared above the Earth, taking in the whole of human accomplishment with my senses and seeing a blank slate, a great grey monument. Five-sided, like a . . .
Like a pentagram.
I remember . . .
I remember freedom to glide, unfettered by mortal constraints, like a little slice of heaven.
I remember the cage.
I remember hearing about it first, about other cages, about broken laws
. . .
I am not bound by your laws . . .
I AM NOT.
. . .
Then why am I here?

ROMULUS:
You're here to provide light.

CANARY:
Kiss me with your sleeping pill eyes, and know my suffering.

REMUS:
No time for kissin'. Not anymore, anyhow. Now sing, please. Unless . . .
                    (He looks around nervously)
Is there a reason for your behavior? Are the glaciers melting? Did the missiles fire? Market crashing? Mass suicides?
I'm kidding. I'm kidding! Kiss all you want. We get a union break. You'll just miss lunch.

ROMULUS:
I haven't kissed anything in . . .
Is this . . . real? Or . . . ?

ROMULUS kisses the CANARY, sweetly. He falters, almost as if struck. REMUS, meanwhile, takes a lunchpail out and begins to eat a ploughman's lunch.

CANARY:
I've suffered for you, since the day I was made . . .

REMUS:
Want a sandwich? Chicken salad.

ROMULUS:
No . . . I . . .

CANARY:
Do you remember?
What was it like?

ROMULUS:
It was . . .
My brain is broken. I can't seem to recall . . . anything from before . . .

REMUS:
Lunch break's over. Diggity-god gams, let's go!

CANARY:
I feel the rhythm of history, do you?
Can you?

REMUS:
Rommy?

ROMULUS:
Coming . . . Reem.

The two begin mining again, occasionally stopping to discard a piece of some broken artifact from all of time and space.

REMUS:
I can tell you're bothered.

ROMULUS:
I'll be all right. If it isn't written down, it isn't real. This is the only reality I need.

134

Boiled Americans

REMUS:
We're doing the Lord's work, here, Rommy. God, guns, and government.
It's a hell of an anthem, wouldn't you say?

ROMULUS:
Hell of a . . .
Yes.

REMUS unearths a slinky.

CANARY:
What's that? It's great!

REMUS:
More to catalogue.

ROMULUS:
It's springy.

CANARY:
It's shiny!

REMUS:
Give it a whirl.

ROMULUS takes the slinky over to a natural carved staircase near the pile of culture, and after a few moments of trying to figure out how it works, sends the slinky down the stairs. It lands in the pile. He looks down at it, and tries to pull it out of the pile, but it is now stuck. He tries again and again, but it will not budge.

CANARY:
What's the matter?

ROMULUS:
It's stuck. I thought . . . only ideas got stuck.
Nothing physical.

REMUS:
As soon as it's discarded, it's relegated to history. You know that. You *should* know that.

ROMULUS has gotten himself tangled up in the slinky while trying to extricate it. He struggles. REMUS goes to help.

REMUS:
You see how dangerous the past is? It binds us. It keeps us from moving forward. That's why it needs to be catalogued, excavated, and ultimately, discarded.

ROMULUS:
This one seems harmless though, like a casserole recipe, or a fancy hat, or—

REMUS:
It's all deception, Rommy. You know better. Believe what you read in the manual. Why would they lie to us?

CANARY:
And now, a moment of education:
Dogma. Noun.
A doctrine, or code of belief accepted as authoritative. A generally held set of formulated beliefs. A blind belief in things, often without a material base.
Note the word belief. How many times does it appear in that definition?
Another:
History. Noun.
The continuum of events occurring in succession leading from the past to the present and even into the future.
Into the future.
Note that nowhere in that definition does the word belief appear.
And yet, doesn't the study of history require an act of faith?
Belief?
After all, who writes history but the winners?
Who believes history, but the descendants of the winners?
If it's written down, it's true. As long as you live in the society that won.

Boiled Americans

The men, now free, dig through the loose ground of their excavation site, pulling out little bits of non-descript culture and discarding them, after appraising some of them briefly.

REMUS:
That's not the kind of talk you should be engaging in, miss.
That kind of talk invites the darkness.

CANARY:
You're wrong.

REMUS:
Ma'am, not to be rude, heaven forbid, but I'm not wrong. This is the way the world is, and you shouldn't question those truths we hold to be self-evident.

CANARY:
Spoken like a true winner.
But I feel . . . something coming.
I . . . don't know if I feel like singing anymore.

ROMULUS:
Do we need to get out? Ventilate the area?

REMUS:
It is dangerous.

CANARY:
. . .
It's . . . always dangerous.
But not now.
Right now it's safe.

She goes back to singing, a bit more reserved now.

ROMULUS:
                        (Unearthing a yo-yo)

I always find the best stuff. Dig it?
> *(He attempts to use the yo-yo)*

REMUS:
Weapon?

ROMULUS:
Probably. Looks like you could take someone's head off at . . .
One . . . two . . . three . . . one and a half paces with this thing.

ROMULUS tosses the yo-yo into the pile. REMUS finds a book. He blows the dust off and looks it over.

REMUS:
Census report.

ROMULUS:
For where?

REMUS looks inside the book.

REMUS:
Earth.
Looks like there were no more pages left.

ROMULUS:
Throw it in the pile. History needs losers too.

REMUS:
Better them than us.

ROMULUS finds an olive branch.

ROMULUS:
Wow, here's an old standard. Haven't needed these in centuries.
At least, if we're talking forward-time.
Backward-time, we might need them again, if the flow doesn't reverse itself.

Boiled Americans

CANARY:
I feel something . . .

REMUS:
Can you believe the world buried beneath? What were they thinking?

CANARY:
Something bad . . .
It's happening.

REMUS:
Thank goodness we're not stuck in the dark ages of war and solitude.

ROMULUS:
Did time stop?

REMUS:
  . . .
What?

ROMULUS:
Are we suspended? Are we still?

CANARY:
It's buried right there, don't open the door.

REMUS:
Come on, keep it up. History won't write itself.

REMUS discovers a small piece of cloth, perhaps gingham.

CANARY:
Don't.

REMUS:
Scraps. Pieces and parts.

CANARY:
You can function because you're detached.
You're wavering dangerously close to the edge of attachment.

ROMULUS:
What's that there?

REMUS:
More junk gone by. Toss it in the pile.

ROMULUS looks at the cloth. REMUS holds it out, still paying attention to the Earth before him.

CANARY:
I would have taken my chances with the hawks and the owls, the freezing winter.
Being down here, mired in the midst of this cultural strip-mining.
This is a death sentence.
Any time we're stripped down to nothing, it's a death sentence.

REMUS: *(without looking)*
That's why you're here.
You're the alarm, only in reverse.
Your silence means death. Darkness. Overtaking everything around you.
You're a holy early warning system.

CANARY:
But it's so hard to be silent. So hard, when there's so much to say.

REMUS holds out the piece of cloth further, making impatient gestures. ROMULUS stares. The CANARY sings lower, softer.

REMUS:
What's the matter? Put it in the pile.
Come on.

ROMULUS:
It looks like . . .

Boiled Americans

Part of a child's dress.
Like my daughter's.
Did I have a daughter?
I can't seem to remember anything before the flash.

REMUS:
Daughters of the revolution. Found their bones years ago, remember?

ROMULUS:
Same pattern, same material. My sense memory is kicking in . . . I forgot
how that felt.

REMUS:
Couldn't possibly be anything related to anything. It's history, dead and
buried. No worries.

ROMULUS:
Dead and . . . ?

REMUS:
Work now. Think later.

*ROMULUS stares at the piece of cloth. He finally takes it from REMUS,
with trembling hands. As he holds it, it bleeds into his hand, more and
more blood. He is visibly upset, and REMUS watches him cautiously.*

ROMULUS:
I
I'm done.
I'm done diggin'.

REMUS:
What?

ROMULUS:
I said I'm done diggin' now.

REMUS:
Can't be. This is all there is to do.

ROMULUS:
I said I'm done. Finished.

ROMULUS drops his pick-axe.

REMUS:
Pick up your pick-axe.

ROMULUS:
 . . .

REMUS:
Pick it up.

ROMULUS:
No.

REMUS:
You know what you're saying? This is your job, this is your duty.

ROMULUS:
It wasn't personal. Before. Time was flowing all regular, and now it's stopped flowing again.
The now is omnipresent.
I am present in this moment, and it has meaning.
IT HAS MEANING.

REMUS:
Doesn't matter. Feelings don't enter into it. If you're not with us, you're with . . . the darkness.
Now:
Pick it up.

ROMULUS, looking distraught, sits on the ground. REMUS looks increasingly concerned and angry about the situation. CANARY sings until further notice.

Boiled Americans

ROMULUS:
She was . . . how old was she?
I can't remember.
I can't remember anything anymore! Where . . .
WHERE DID IT ALL GO?

REMUS:
It's not your job to remember. It's your job to mine the sins and triumphs, to record history through wrecking history. We re-write by renovation.
> *(REMUS tries to force ROMULUS to take the pick)*
Take it. Get up.

ROMULUS:
NO!

ROMULUS pushes REMUS, who falters, and then attacks with ferocity. The two men fight, struggling over everything and nothing, rolling on the ground. CANARY sings louder, her song coming to a huge climax, beautiful but ear-splittingly loud. REMUS gets the best of ROMULUS and grabs the pick-axe, holding it over ROMULUS, about to murder him. After a tense moment, the lights flicker. CANARY stops singing, silent and still. The men, breathing heavily, calm down. REMUS drops the pick and slumps against a wall. They look at one another, then slowly get to their feet. ROMULUS picks up the cloth, and sadly moves it to the pile, never looking at REMUS.

ROMULUS:
I don't know where I am anymore.
> *(He looks at the blood, covering his arm.)*
Is this mine?
Or hers?
. . .
Yours?

REMUS:
I don't have any blood. I'm dry as a bone.

The dust down here dries up all the moisture. Sucks it out of you like a vampire.

The lights flicker and a few go out. It is darker now, shadows are longer.

ROMULUS:
Do you smell anything? Taste anything in the air?

REMUS:
Can't. Odorless. Tasteless. Can't even feel it with your sixth sense. That's why we need the canary. Warning.

ROMULUS:
Warnings come all the time. All those things we found . . .
Do you think those people had a canary?

REMUS:
I don't know.

REMUS helps ROMULUS to his feet.

ROMULUS:
Do you think the darkness found them?
Or do you think they . . . invited it?
        (He wipes some of the blood off his arm.)
If blood could speak . . .
It would cry out. It would bubble up and cry out.
Spilled in defiance of those who sent it out to wet the land.

REMUS:
Too dry in here for that.

ROMULUS:
Listen.

They listen. There is total silence. REMUS finally looks to see CANARY, still motionless and silent.

Boiled Americans

REMUS:
Canary's dead.

They stare at her body.

ROMULUS:
. . .
Now what?

(They look at each other.)

REMUS:
Now we leave.

ROMULUS:
But . . .
There's nowhere to go?
Everywhere's the same.
Land won't be habitable.
Irradiated.

REMUS:
That's what the canary is for.

ROMULUS:
You can't wait til' she dies to heed the warning. It's too late then.

REMUS:
No, we have to go!

ROMULUS:
You go, I'll stay here.

REMUS:
That's what she's for. If the bird stops singing, the mine's not safe. That's the rule.

ROMULUS: *(far away)*
I am not bound by your laws . . .

REMUS:
There's no way out after I pull up the ladder.

ROMULUS:
Longest ladder in the world. It'll just end up down here in the pile.
The next pair of miners will find it. They'll laugh and pick it apart, and throw it away.
And their canary will sing silence.
And the world's canary will sing silence.

REMUS:
We have to go. Now.
                    (He takes a few steps)
Your history will die here. Now.

ROMULUS:
It's already dead.
I can't remember it. It's not written down.

REMUS just stares for a long beat, then begins to whistle/sing softly, like the CANARY had. He exits. ROMULUS sits for a long moment, then gets up and walks to the CANARY. He looks her over, walks back to the pile and reaches in. He pulls and struggles, unable to extricate anything from it. He tries again, exhausting himself. Finally, with one monstrous pull, he comes out with a handful of coins. ROMULUS crosses to CANARY, and picks up her body, placing her gently in the digging area. He takes two of the coins and places them over her eyes. He covers her lightly with some of the soil. ROMULUS then crosses the pile, as more of the lights go out around them. He strips down to his underwear, and lies down on the pile.

Boiled Americans

and here　it comes
　　　　　still at spe
　　　　　　　ed some
　　　　　　　　　how an
　　　　　　　　　　　d it sma
　　　　　　　　　　shes th
　　　　　　　　　　　rough a
　　　　　　　　　　　　ll the pa　　　　　\
　　　　　　　　　　　　　ranoia- *dead*
　　　　　　　　　　　　　　　　　　　/

Michael Allen Rose

Case File 022

*[Ripped and torn from the appendix of the oldest book in the internal affairs library: The repeating Angel Number 22 is a message from your angels to maintain your convictions and keep an optimistic outlook and a **positive attitude** as your desires are currently being manifested for you.]*

• Earlier Sunday afternoon, three people were shot within blocks of each other in the Eden Green neighborhood on the ~~Far~~ (STOP IT! STOP!) South Side; officials said at least two of the shootings were related. A man, 43, was shot in the chest, and a woman, 22, was shot in the foot and leg near 132nd Street and Prairie Avenue around 3:30 p.m. Both were typical Americans. Both of them had pet bullets when they were children. Both of them bought Bullet of the Month Club memberships, which came with a free calendar of bullet pictures, taken by bullets.

The Metatron said the shootings stemmed from a domestic dispute. Police said both were taken to Advocate Christ Medical Center and are expected to recover from their wounds.

Around the same time, at 3:10 p.m., firefighters were called to the Little Calumet River at 134th Street and South Vernon Avenue. But arriving crews were told by police that a person had been taken into custody. The man was chased by officers because he had a weapon. The weapon was not an axe, or a knife. It was not a candlestick, a rope, a lead pipe or a spanner. It was bullets. They came from a gun. It went bang. It was not known if he was a suspect in the shootings on Prairie or another shooting an hour earlier in the 13100 block of South Forrestville Avenue.

In that shooting, a woman, 66, a typical

Boiled Americans

American, was grazed on the top of the head as she walked up the steps of her porch in the Golden Gate neighborhood. The woman had just parked her car when she heard shots, according to the Metatron. "At the top of the stairs, she felt something on the top of her head."

She went to Roseland Hospital, but it was unclear who drove her. It might have been a speeding bullet. The thing that she felt on the top of her head was not a fancy hat fresh from the haberdashery.

"She was not the intended target," the police lieutenant said, adding she was an "unfortunate victim."

That's all right. Unfortunate victims don't spray guilt from their thorax like a stinkbug toward predators. The police are armed with military grade super weapons. We, the typical Americans, the parasites, crawl into the barrels of their guns and wait for the bang. But, these typical Americans were all unfortunate victims. Not terrorists, right? Not enemy combatants, right? Surely not enemies of the American way, right?

They probably got in the way. Like kids running after a ball across a busy street. Too many typical Americans chase their toys across the bullet highway. They say they just want to live their lives, but we know better, don't we?

They were probably angry. Disenfranchised. Poor. Colored. Deviant. Sexually confused. Unemployed. They got in the way. Bang. They shouldn't have done what they did. Bang. If you think it's the fault of the finger that's fucking that trigger so softly, so sensually, you're fooling yourself. Bang. We know what's up. We watch TV.

Bang. Bang. Bang.

XXXV. Final Billing and Damages Done

And finally: lo, The Metatron speaks: "A wop-bop aloo-bop, a lop bam boom." I look to the translators, but they are all dead, buried up to their necks in shame, silver dollar pancakes stapled over their eyes.

Was this the wisdom we were waiting for? Segundo Morris comes up behind me and puts a bag over my head. I don't need to see him to know he looks exactly like me.

The knife plunges into my side, needle thin, severing the liminal space between the sacred inside and the invading sombre air of the outside. A whirlwind, a maelstrom, sucking air into the core.

A spray of teeth washed up on shore like the subversion of a media empire, a barrel of monkeys, inverted.

Silence. Nothing. There are no further words; we are left without meaning, language insignificant beside the act of acting, the choice to choose, man's ruin, the thudding heart-beating alligator clip of our demise. I scream one single word: "entropy." The end is mercy. I breathe in stagnant iron; I turn to rust, the screaming echoes silent across the void as The Metatron reveals itself to be a blind idiot god, a ham-fisted man-child of omnipresent proportions. Cosmic drool dribble-drips, splashing and drowning the plebeians. The books burn like stars.

Solutions are imperfect, fleeting.

"O God, please destroy us all." The prayer goes up from a thousand nihilistic lips, sprayed like acid saliva through gritted teeth the size of moon craters. Segundo Morris: My doppelganger, my lover, my clone, my nightmare, I am dragged away kicking and cursing into someone's neighborhood, where I am forced in the moment to live out every single day in complete and utter starvation. The food desert of firing squads. A lethal injection of sanity, rolling out like cookie dough, pumping from deep beneath the Earth until the only sound is a single gunshot, penetrating even the whitest shade of nothing.

Boiled Americans

[XXXXREDACTEDXXXX]

Bonus Material

Appendix 1: Mortality Divination Chart

Use this handy chart to determine the date of your own death as you read.

Use pencil to ensure accuracy.

	001-003	004-006	007-012	013-014	015-016	017-019	020-021	022
I-III								
IV-VI	null						sq.	
VII-X								
XI-XV								
XVI-XVIII				rec.				
XIX-XXI								
XXII-XXV								
XXVI-XXIX						æt. (13)		
XXX-XXXI								
XXXII-XXXV								

Appendix 2: A love letter

Dear Detroit,

How are you? I am fine. Yesterday, we scraped the remains of ten homeless brains off the bean! The mayor calls it his "Cleaning Up the City initiative." Brains are super sticky! I bet they're delicious. Rarrr! I am the city that eats brains! Rarrr! LOL J/K!!! Can you imagine?How is the weather where you are? Our air is cleaner than yours, but filled with meat. It tastes like death here. I bet you can relate! Have you heard anything from New York lately? I'm a little worried that the murder rate is going to go down again, and then the tourist supply will choke the streets. Gross! Don't you wish we had throats to clear? Hack hack hack, oh no, there's a tourist in my throat! Quick, shoot it! Haha!Anyway, I just wanted to drop you a line and say I'm thinking about you. Once all the parasites have been dealt with, maybe we can take a vacation together or something. I'd like to intertwine smokestacks, if you know what I mean (and I think you do—ROTFLOL!). Stay awesome and don't forget to dodge!

Love,
Chicago

About the Author

Michael Allen Rose is a writer, musician and performer based in Chicago IL. He's been seen in a variety of places, doing a variety of things. He's written books like *Party Wolves in My Skull*, appeared in publications like the *Magazine of Bizarro Fiction* and released albums under the name Flood Damage. You can check some of them out following him around at www.michaelallenrose.com. He's not often nearly as afraid as he should be.

All Art is Junk by R. A. Harris

Lana Rivers, a girl with paintbrush hair, is missing and it's up to Lancelot, her cyborg knight, and his bionic conjoined twin, Cilia, to find her before her evil father, a disrespected artist turned mad-scientist, performs a terrible experiment on her.

Cherub by David C. Hayes

Cherub wasn't like the other boys—too slow, too rough—but he didn't deserve what that hospital did to him, and now he will make them pay.

Skinners by Adam Millard

Los Angeles, the City of Angels. At least, that's what the brochure says. What it fails to mention is the earthquakes. Oh, and the flesh-eating creatures lying dormant beneath the concrete, waiting for the chance to surface once again. Their wait is over . . .

The After-Life Story of Pork Knuckles Malone by MP Johnson

What's a farm boy to do when his pet pig becomes an evil, decaying hunk of ham with slime-spewing psychic powers?

A Lightbulb's Lament by Grant Wamack

A gentleman with a lightbulb for head wakes up in a world full of darkness, hooks up with a beautiful ex-prostitute, and an old man who can heal people; he travels down south to find the mysterious Creator.

The Horror Show by Vincenzo Bilof

A poetry novel—a narcoleptic, amnesiac Nobel Prize-winning poet becomes the subject of an experiment to cure madness.

Beyond by Jordan Krall

From Jerusalem to Mars, psychiatry and the unraveling of the universe

Gravity Comics Massacre
by Vincenzo Bilof

An absolutely shitty novella involving comic books, aliens, a serial killer, teenagers in an abandoned town, horror-trope dream sequences, and an ending you're going to hate.

Glue by Scott Lange

Sticky bowels and sticky situations.

Ascent by Matthew Bialer

Is the 8 foot tall creature haunting a small town in Iowa in the fall of the year 1903 the product of a hoax and collective imagination or was it one of the first documented paranormal event in America? This epic poem grapples with these questions.

Fecal Terror by David Bernstein

A killer turd is on the loose!

The Fairy Princess of Trains
by Christopher Boyle

Danny's mediocre life turns upside-down when his couch starts whispering to him. Then he's charged with a supernatural mission: Rescue the Fairy Princess of Trains.

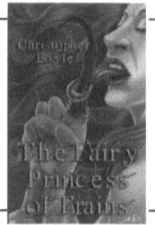

Terence, Mephisto & Viscera Eyes
by Chris Kelso

9 new science fiction stories from Chris Kelso

How to Succesfully Kidnap Strangers by Max Booth III

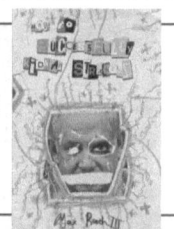

Do not respond to bad reviews. If you must respond to bad reviews, please do not kidnap the reviewer.

Bizarro Bizarro: An Anthology

The finest bizarro short stories from 2013.

Necrosaurus Rex by Nicolas Day

Necrosaurus Rex tells the tale of Martin, a simple janitor, who takes an unfortunate trip through time, becomes a violent mutant, and the father of us all. There's 14 billion years crushed inside these pages, and most of them are pretty nasty.

Day of the Milkman by S. T. Cartledge

In a world dominated by the milk industry, only one milkman survives after a terrible storm sinks all the ships and throws the Great White Sea out of balance.

Moosejaw Frontier by Chris Kelso

An unapologetic disaster of metafiction

Notes from the Guts of a Hippo by Grant Wamack

A rugged journalist travels to Brazil in search of a missing hippo researcher and the notes left behind lead to something earth shatteringly revelatory.

Industrial Carpet Drag by Bruce Taylor

Chemicals make you do great things!

ADHD Vampire by Matthew Vaughn

He came, he conquered, he was distracted a lot